Rosie's War

Also by Ann Carroll

Rosie's War

Ann Carroll

POOLBEG
FOR CHILDREN

Published 2002
Poolbeg Press Ltd.
123 Grange Hill, Baldoyle,
Dublin 13, Ireland
Email: poolbeg@poolbeg.com

13 5 7 9 10 8 6 4 2

A catalogue record for this book is available from the British Library.

ISBN 1-84223-0735

Cover designed by DW Design
Typeset by Patricia Hope in Goudy 11/14.8
Printed by Cox & Wyman

www.poolbeg.com

About the Author

Ann Carroll is married, with two children, and lives in Dublin. For many years she was a teacher of English in Killinarden Community School but has recently given up teaching to become a full-time writer.

She is the author of four other books in the *Rosie* series, and has also written *Amazing Grace* and *Laura Delaney's Deadliest Day*.

Acknowledgements

For permission to use lyrics of "We'll Meet Again" (words & music Parker/Charles) Copyright @ 1939 Dash Music Co. LTD, 8/9 Frith St, London W.1

For my brother, George O'Hara,
whose memories of 1943 were a great help.

Chapter 1

It just wasn't fair, Rosie McGrath thought. Her parents were rotten, leaving her in the middle of July with a childminder – a *childminder*, for Heaven's sake! – while they went off gallivanting in Paris for a week.

"No, you can't come with us," Dad told her. "It's a business trip. We'll be working all day every day."

"No, you can't go to Helena's," Mum said. "I know she's your best friend, but you've stayed with her too often and I don't want to impose on her mother again. The woman will think you're neglected."

"Well, I *am* neglected," Rosie wailed and, seeing her mother's look of guilt, added, "and I'm not trusted either. Why can't I stay here on my own?"

"Because you're too young!" both parents answered.

Still feeling in the wrong, Mum tried to persuade, "Look, Rosie! You know your gran won't be home from her holiday with Uncle Jack for a few weeks. You know too that we can't leave you to look after yourself at thirteen. You're not old enough."

"Which is why," Dad cut in, "we've got you a really good

1

baby-sitter – oops! I mean childminder. The agency assured us Caroline Mooney is an experienced young woman and very serious about her job. So no more arguments, Rosie!"

And that was that.

What the agency hadn't told her parents was that the childminder was also a maniac, at least as far as junk – which Caroline called 'antiques'- was concerned. Every day she dragged her charge into town, down lanes and alleyways to look in poky shops that had been there for centuries, owned by people who seemed just as ancient, with their pale parchment skin and watery eyes.

Rosie wouldn't have minded so much if there'd been anything interesting in these shops, like gold and silver coins or fabulous jewellery. But as far as she could see, they were filled with rubbish – rickety chairs, broken delph, mouldy pictures. The places were always dark and dusty, smelling of cabbage and damp. But Caroline loved them, entering each shop as if it were an Aladdin's Cave, poring for hours over the foxed pages of old books or searching for a signature on a gloomy oil painting. Rosie began to think her childminder was as cracked as some of the vases she studied so intently.

It mightn't have been so bad if the sun hadn't decided to shine every day in a cloudless sky.

"Can I go to the beach with my friend Helena?" Rosie had asked on one of those perfect days.

"I'm afraid not. You might get sunstroke, or be stung by a jellyfish. Then what would your parents say?" She wasn't joking. The agency was right about how seriously Caroline took her job. She wouldn't let Rosie out of her sight for a minute in case something happened to her.

The week passed very slowly, but it passed.

On Thursday afternoon, the day before her parents were due home, Rosie hallucinated about blue seas and white sand as they traipsed along a hot cobbled lane off Clanbrassil Street. 'It's not fair!' she brooded. 'Mum and Dad left me with a lunatic. I'd run away if they weren't coming home tomorrow – and if they hadn't promised me a *big* present. They'd better deliver.'

Caroline turned into a shop and Rosie followed. Sighing, she shut the door behind her, locking out the sunshine. "More junk," she muttered. By now she knew Caroline's routine. The childminder would want to examine everything, peering under boxes and tables, holding objects up to the non-existent light, running her fingers over pieces of china.

Rosie sat gingerly on the broken seat of a cane chair, moaning to herself.

On a small table in front of her was a battered suitcase with broken catches. Idly she lifted the lid. She yawned at the contents: a yellowing newspaper and a large notebook with the word *Ledger* embossed on the cover in faded gold. Nothing more. Boring!

She saw the childminder turn the jug this way and that. 'Oh God, we'll be here for ages,' she thought. Taking up the notebook she flicked through the first few pages. There were a lot of numbers in neat rows. Rosie recognised the signs for pounds, shillings and pence and guessed it was some kind of old accounts book. She yawned again and glanced up.

Caroline was now examining a painting with the aid of a small magnifying glass, looking for a famous signature that the shop owner might have missed.

"It has happened, you know," she'd told Rosie earnestly

when the girl had wanted to know why they had to spend every glorious day in such places. "People do find lost masterpieces. I read in a magazine about this couple who saw a Ming vase in a museum and it was exactly like one they'd bought in a market. It turned out theirs wasn't a copy. It was the real thing and it sold for millions at a New York auction. Which was nice for them because they'd been very poor. They were so lucky, because they'd been about to drill a hole in the vase and turn it into a lamp and then it would have been worthless!"

For an hour or so afterwards Rosie had been fired with the notion of making her fortune and had eagerly examined everything in the next junk shop. But she had driven Caroline mad, asking, "What about this table? It looks at least two hundred years old. What about this box? I think it's silver. And look at this cup, Caroline! There's so much dust on it! It has to be ancient."

At first the childminder had tried to be patient, glad to have someone sharing her enthusiasm. But she faltered a bit when Rosie mistook a crack on an ornament for an important mark. And she finally snapped when her charge, in a state of great excitement, summoned her to look at a sculpted head. "It's bronze. And I can see the signature on it," Rosie whispered. "You said Rodin is famous. I want half of whatever we make."

So certain was she that Caroline's eyes brightened with hope and she hurried over. She wiped the signature clean of dust and frowned.

"For heaven's sake, Rosie!" she said. "*Rodin* indeed! *R O Dinneen* is what's written here. And can you not tell the difference between painted plaster and bronze? *Please!* Stop helping me."

Rosie had given up, not without relief. It was very tedious work trying to make a fortune.

Now, out of boredom, Rosie glanced at the newspaper. It was dated Thursday, 19th July, 1943. Beside the main report was a photo of a man in a suit. He was standing inside a garden gate and he was handcuffed to a garda. Rosie found the headline vaguely interesting:

BUSINESSMAN CHARGED WITH MURDER

At least more interesting than junk. Then, as she read, her nerves tingled with shock:

Yesterday evening the businessman Edward O'Neill was arrested on suspicion of the murder of Michael Donovan, who disappeared one year ago.

The victim was a joint partner with the twin brothers Edward and Henry O'Neill, in the import/export firm, Donovan O'Neill.

The company was started in 1900, though not under its present name, by the prominent businessman, Joseph O'Neill, father of the suspect. The firm was a source of great family pride, with offices in Dublin, Cork and also in Zurich, where Henry O'Neill now runs the European branch. In recent times however there have been some financial problems.

Following information, police found Michael Donovan's remains at a lonely spot in the Dublin Mountains. A wallet recovered at the scene helped identification. Detectives arrived at Edward O'Neill's home, 35 Griffith Avenue, around 10 pm on Friday where they removed various items of evidence. As his wife, Maria, and son, Patrick (13) looked on in shock, the businessman was led away in handcuffs and taken to Whitehall Garda Station for questioning.

While a motive for murder is not yet established, it is rumoured that Mr Donovan had been responsible for some heavy losses at the firm and this resulted in many heated arguments with the suspect.

There was no doubt in Rosie's mind. This was the Edward O'Neill she had met in 1900 on her last journey to the past. There couldn't be two sets of twins with the same names and whose father was called Joseph.

In 1900 Edward was twelve. Rosie remembered the adventurous, mischievous boy. He'd been great fun, always ready for a laugh. He'd also been brave and had planned the rescue of his twin from the kidnapper, Donnelly. There was no way he could have grown up to be a murderer!

"I wonder what happened after his arrest?" Rosie murmured. Surely he must have been found innocent. Henry probably came home and sorted it out. But what if he didn't? The idea of the boy she'd known having to spend years in jail was awful.

Her face pale, Rosie stared into the shadows of the small shop.

"What has you so interested?" Caroline's voice interrupted her thoughts. "I thought you'd be doing a road-runner out that door once you saw I'd finished. What *are* you reading that's got you so hooked?"

"Oh, just an old paper," Rosie mumbled. There was no way she could tell Caroline about Edward. Rosie tried to imagine the childminder's response if she said, "I know the murder suspect mentioned in this paper. You see I met him in 1900." She'd probably think Rosie had managed to get sunstroke in spite of her best efforts and she'd make her go to bed the minute they got home.

"July 1943," Caroline looked at the date and laughed "I hope you don't think this is valuable? It may be old but it's worthless. It's about to fall apart. See!" She blew and the front page shed its edges.

"Don't do that," Rosie jumped up. "I'm going to buy it anyway!" Then seeing Caroline's look of disbelief, she muttered, "It'll come in handy at school. History projects and that."

The childminder was bewildered. In the short time she'd known Rosie, the girl had mentioned school only once and that was to say it'd be a great place if there were no teachers, no rules and no work. Certainly she didn't seem the type who'd plan projects during her summer holidays.

While Caroline was digesting this surprise, Rosie made for the counter, the newspaper flaking a little in her grip.

"Ah," the owner said silkily, "you opened the old case. I bought it at a police auction hoping it might contain something valuable – not that the newspaper isn't of some value. Indeed you have an eye for a bargain. Emergency papers are rare, you know."

"I don't want it for an emergency," said Rosie, wondering what he was on about.

The shopkeeper laughed as if she'd said something really witty. "Oh, we will have our little joke, Miss. That'll be five pounds, please."

"I hope that's a little joke too," Caroline, arriving at the counter, butted in. "Five pounds! It's not worth five pence. Look at the paper! It's crumbling."

"Then she can use it as confetti," the man snapped. He knew Caroline's type. Spent half a day in the shop and bought nothing. But Rosie was different. He guessed she wanted that newspaper at all costs. And he was right. Before there were any more objections, she handed over the money.

"Well, I hope you give a refund if it's not satisfactory!" was all Caroline could say.

"Don't be silly, love." He was sneering now, sure of his sale. "That oul paper will be a bag of crumbs in no time. I'm telling you, it's only good for a wedding!"

But Rosie was already out the door, the newspaper gingerly placed in the old plastic bag he'd given her. All Caroline could do was follow.

Rosie was very quiet at dinner time. Usually she raised fierce objections to Caroline's healthy cooking, having a natural dislike for cabbage and turnips, stew or mackerel. And her minder put the oddest things together, always saying, "This will give you iron and other vital minerals, so that when you're an adult you'll be big and strong." The image of a wrestler would pop into Rosie's mind. She had no desire to be big and strong. In fact, she wasn't at all eager to be an adult if it meant eating Caroline's vile cooking. Thank heavens Mum would be home the next day.

But now she didn't even notice the barely poached egg – "so good for you, all runny" – arranged in the middle of a mound of broccoli and mushy peas. She ate them without a murmur.

"Are you feeling okay, Rosie? You seem to like your dinner."

"I was just wondering, Caroline, if a person were found guilty of murder, would they spend long in jail? I mean, in –"

The childminder sniffed, "Are you being smart? I know

you don't like my cooking, but it won't kill you. I'm not trying to poison you, as you keep hinting. There's no need to go over the top!"

"What?" For a second Rosie looked puzzled, then she giggled. "I wasn't getting at your dinner. I ate it, didn't I, whatever it was? I just want to know this: say a person in 1943 was found guilty of murder, would he have spent a long time in jail?"

"No, not long. Maybe a week, maybe two. Then he was hanged." Caroline was blunt, still feeling insulted.

"Hanged?" Rosie gulped.

"Yes. Once the jury found him guilty, the judge always said, 'Would the prisoner please rise.'" Caroline warmed to the subject. "Then the judge put on his black cap that he kept especially for death sentences and said something like, 'You have been found guilty of murder and I therefore sentence you to death. You will be taken to a place of execution on such and such a date and hanged by the neck until you are dead. May God have mercy on your soul.' After that the executioner arrived from England and, on the day, the prisoner was brought to the hanging house in the prison yard. He climbed the steps to the wooden scaffold and he stood over a trapdoor." Caroline paused for a moment, relishing her description. Then she continued, "The executioner made sure one end of the rope was tied properly to the crossbeam and he placed the noose around the murderer's throat and put a white sack over his head. At the appointed time, he pushed a lever, the trapdoor fell and the prisoner dropped into space. He was either strangled or his neck broke, or maybe both. I'm not sure."

Rosie put a hand to her own neck, throat tightening.

She had to take a deep breath before she could ask, "Why did the executioner come from England? Would no Irish person do the job?"

"That wasn't the reason. Ireland has only a small population and there were hardly any murders then, so there wasn't much work here in the hanging line."

She stopped, then informed Rosie, "The last executioner ever in Britain and Ireland was a man called Pierrepoint. You should remember that. It can come in handy at quizzes."

"Hanging must be horrible," Rosie said.

"I'm sure it is," Caroline nodded. "For the victim anyway. It was quite popular with audiences, I believe."

"Audiences!"

"Oh yes. Years and years ago there were public hangings and crowds went to see them."

"That wasn't very nice." Rosie felt faint.

"No, well we're more civilised these days, which is just as well since there's a lot more murders. If there were a death penalty now, there'd be loads of people hanged!."

"And were there public hangings in 1943?" Rosie couldn't bear the idea of Edward having to face a scaffold *and* a crowd.

"Executions took place in prisons at that stage. I suppose people had become a bit more humane. Well, that's if you don't count the war."

All of a sudden Rosie wanted to stop talking about prisons and hangings. It was making her sick, especially when she thought of Edward. What if his innocence hadn't been proved? What if the worst had happened? What if Henry hadn't been able to help?

She imagined the boy she'd known climbing the steps of

the scaffold, his face white. Of course in 1943 he was a man of fifty-five, not a youngster, but she could only see him as a boy and the image was unbearable.

Caroline was glad of the lull. She had a lot to do before she could take her holidays next day. She made a mental list while Rosie sat in silence, her heart heavy.

Finally Rosie made her decision. 'I'll have to go back,' she thought. 'I have to help Edward.' She swallowed. What if she couldn't help? The notion was too horrible and she pushed it away. 'I have to at least *try* and find out what happened. Then maybe I can change things.'

Chapter 2

"I want to get in a few messages for your parents, so we'll have to use the late store," Caroline said some time later.

"May I stay here?" Rosie said and the childminder hesitated. Then she looked at the girl's strained face and her heart sank. Surely Rosie wasn't going to get ill the day before her parents came home?

"I'm a bit tired," Rosie was plaintive.

"All right, though I don't like to leave you on your own."

Rosie felt like a four-year-old, but she wanted Caroline to go so that she could think and plan in peace. "You'll only be gone an hour at the most. It's not enough time for me to go wild. I'm hardly going to organise a party!" Catching the childminder's anxiety, she added quickly, "Only joking."

"Well, you're not to open the door and you're not to talk to strangers, d'you hear?"

"How can I talk to strangers if I don't open the door, or maybe you think they'll come in the window!" Then seeing the other's alarm, she said, "That's a joke too. I'm just going to sit here and rest."

At last Caroline was gone.

Rosie took the newspaper from the plastic bag and spread it out carefully on the table.

There was a lot in it about the Second World War, especially about the invasion of Sicily by the Allied Forces. Also there were listings for the cinemas and theatres; old-fashioned ads for shops done in pen and ink; warnings about spies; articles on the danger of Eire being drawn into the war, one of which caught her attention:

If Eire wishes to stay out of this war we cannot allow spies to operate here. Nor should we give out any information that would make us appear to take sides. This would place our country in great danger, leaving us open to attack by either Britain or Germany.

Mr Churchill, the British Prime Minister, has already demanded the use of our ports for Britain's war efforts and has hinted that these could be taken by force. While we should not be frightened by Mr Churchill's threats, neither should we give him the excuse he may be looking for: that we are siding with the enemy.

Therefore as citizens it is our duty to report any suspicions we may have which could lead to the arrest and internment of spies during the Emergency.

The word *Emergency* with a capital E appeared often in the newspaper. It seemed to describe the war in Ireland. Rosie looked it up in her mum's dictionary in case she had misunderstood its meaning: *Emergency: an urgent situation needing immediate attention.*

"That's what Dad says when he thinks I use the telephone too much. Or Mum, when she sees my school reports. It doesn't seem a proper word for the Second World War!"

She studied the four pages, but saw nothing further about the murder. Rereading the report, she could see little hope for Edward. If the police had taken evidence of the crime from his home then he must have been convicted. She would have to go back! Yet how could she? Her parents would be home next day and there was no way she could disappear for any length of time without their knowledge.

"Mum, Dad, I'm going on a trip to 1943," she said aloud and giggled, imagining the reply:

'Yes, dear, well don't forget to take your rain coat,' her mum would say, if she weren't properly listening, which was often the case, while her dad would just raise his newspaper a little higher and tell her, 'You've been watching too many films, my girl. You need a healthy pastime, like mowing the lawn.' He was always trying to get her to mow the lawn, or wash his car, or clean up the garage on the grounds that these activities were good for her health.

As she pondered the problem, the phone rang. It was her mum from Paris.

"Rosie, your father and I have a dinner appointment, so I can't talk for long. How would you feel if we didn't come home for another week?"

"Another week!" Rosie could hardly believe it.

"We'll make it up to you, I promise." Her mother sounded really guilty and went on in a rush, "It's just that we have the opportunity to make a really good business deal, but it will take a week to sort out the details."

Mind racing, Rosie said nothing and Mrs McGrath began to sound wretched, "Look, I know it's hard on you and we'll have to do something really nice in return. Please try and understand –"

"Oh, I do, Mum. It's okay, really." Rosie's heart soared as she realised the possibilities.

"I knew you would," said her mother. "You're wonderful! Now, let me speak to Caroline."

"Caroline?"

"Yes. She'll have to stay on for another week, if possible."

The girl swallowed, "She's not here, Mum. She's gone to the shops. And she can't stay another week. She's going to Connemara tomorrow for a fortnight's holiday with her sister."

For a moment there was silence, then her mum sighed, "We'll have to come back, so. You can't stay in the house on your own."

Rosie struggled for ideas, then, "But I don't have to stay here. Caroline and I are getting on really well –" this was a downright lie–"and she was saying how beautiful Connemara was and how she'd love me to see it and wasn't it a pity I couldn't go with her. Honest, Mum. She'd love to take me with her."

It would have been more truthful to say Caroline would prefer to fall into a barrel of superglue than take Rosie on holiday. But then she could hardly tell Mum what she actually intended doing, could she? And they were only white lies really, since they were in a good cause.

Mum was understandably suspicious, if hopeful, "Last time I rang, you didn't like Caroline. If I remember properly, you said a bit of her brain was missing. Are you sure you want to go on holiday with her? Are you sure she wants to take you? Absolutely certain?"

Rosie caught the tone. Her mother was longing to believe her. She took a chance. "Of course I am. She's really interesting, especially about public hangings. And she practically invited me. You can ask her yourself. She'll be back in half an hour."

"Public hangings? No! Don't tell me – I don't have time. Actually I'm in an awful hurry, Rosie. Our taxi is arriving any minute. So I can't ring back and talk to Caroline." Her mother started rushing, "Now we'll be home on the afternoon flight tomorrow week. It arrives in at 4pm. For some reason the morning plane is booked up. How will you get home from Connemara? Tell Caroline to have a good holiday! Do you want us to collect you? Have you got her holiday phone number?"

"I'll get the train home, Mum. Caroline will organise everything." Rosie took advantage of her mother's mad hurry and ignored her last question. "Can you hear me? Mum? Mum? The line's gone all funny. I'll see you in a week, Mum, if you can hear me! You know Caroline will look after me. I'd better go. Have a nice dinner!"

Rosie hung up, ignoring her mother's shouts at the other end. Holding her breath, she listened to the silence. Then, as realisation struck her, she did a dance of relief and anticipation. "There's nothing to stop me going back now!" she thought. "I can't wait to see Edward again."

When Caroline returned, Rosie said truthfully, "Mum rang. She says they have to finish some business, so they won't be home on the morning flight."

The childminder looked dismayed, "But I'm getting the midday train! What time will they be home then?"

"The plane gets in at 4 o'clock." As Caroline began to groan, Rosie added, "It's all right though. I told Mum you'd be gone and she wasn't a bit upset. She said to tell you to enjoy your holiday. Of course she knows I can manage."

Caroline looked doubtful. But she was really looking

forward to a break. Rosie hadn't been the easiest person to mind, arguing every step of the way, bored with antiques, giving out about her cooking . . . It would be nice to have a holiday.

She made up her mind. "Well, you'll only have to wait a few hours so I suppose you'll be all right. And if your mum doesn't mind, who am I to object? Anyway, I'll leave my phone number so she can ring me."

While the childminder was packing, Rosie went to her bedroom. The trip to 1943 had to be carefully planned. She was about to travel back almost sixty years and she had to be properly prepared. She looked at the date on her watch – Thursday 12th July – at least the time of year was right. She would arrive almost a week before Edward was arrested. Hopefully she would find a way to help, to change the past once more.

Taking up a notebook she jotted down what she would need:

1. *Something belonging to Edward that will give me a link to his time*
2. *Something from the present that could be useful*
3. *My watch*
4. *Food*
5. *A gift for Edward*

And that was it.

At the back of her bedside locker she found the photograph she'd brought back from 1900. Although her mum and gran would have been so interested, she could never show it to them since they did not believe in time-travel. It would cause too many problems.

Now she looked intently at the sepia print, at Joseph,

whom she'd met in Oak Park in 1870 and again in 1900. He was Gran's great-uncle and he was the only person Rosie had ever met who'd also journeyed through time. He stared out at her from the picture, seated beside Louisa, his wife. Standing behind them were the twin boys, Edward and Henry. In the fashion of the day, none of them smiled, yet they looked happy and Rosie remembered a close, contented family. She smiled at the short inscription Joseph had written on the back.

This was her link to Edward. She wrapped the photo carefully before placing it in her haversack.

She tried to think what she could bring from the present that might be useful in 1943. When she'd first met Joseph, she'd had with her a small but powerful tape recorder. Last time it had been a CD player. In 1920 she'd used a camera. And on every visit she'd worn her digital watch, with its date and calculator. She would wear it again this time. It was essential to her journey, but she wanted to take something else as well.

Pondering, she caught the glint of steel in her wardrobe and eyed her Rollerblades doubtfully. "Well, I can't think of anything else and I suppose they could come in handy. I'll take them!"

What about food? The newspaper had mentioned coupons and ration cards, so there must have been shortages. She did a list. Coffee. Mum found it impossible to get through the day without at least four cups of coffee, so that ought to go down well. And tea, in case anyone liked that. And sugar. Some of the masses of fruit Caroline had bought. And the big bag of unpopped corn at the back of the cupboard.

Tomorrow, when Caroline was gone, she would pack the food. And she could use her pocket money to buy sweets in the morning. Caroline hadn't let her spend a penny, nagging, "There's plenty of nourishing food in the house. You don't need ice cream or sweets. They'll only rot your teeth." Such a pain! Still, it was useful to have some money now.

That left item number 5. What gift could she bring Edward? As a boy he'd loved everything to do with war. He'd owned regiments of toy soldiers and spoke of battle-plans and tactics. He'd also loved all her stories of the future, seeing it as a bright and magical place. She should take something for him that was right up to the minute. He would like nothing better than her Game-Player, with its six-inch screen and *Star Wars* discs. Rosie slipped it into the haversack.

She knew there was no point bringing clothes. The distant past, in her experience, was no place for jeans and tops. Anything modern would cause too many awkward questions. And what she wore tomorrow would change the instant she returned to the past. Recalling the drawings of frocks in the newspaper ads, she sighed, "Oh God, I'm going to look *so hideous!*"

But she was all set and she could hardly wait for the next day, when her adventure would begin.

Chapter 3

At last Caroline was gone. Conscientious to the end, she had given Rosie a long list of things to do, afraid she would get into mischief before her parents returned.

"*Clean out under the stairs,*" the girl read with disbelief. "*Dust and polish furniture in parents' room. Hoover front room again. Clean silverware. Tidy presses in the kitchen. Make nice welcome-home card for parents. Polish all shoes belonging to parents.*"

Rosie felt hysterical. "Polish their shoes!" she muttered. "If I did that, they'd be asking *why* for the next year. They'd think I must've done something awful and was trying to make up for it. And look at all the work she's given me! It'd take four days, not four hours!" The girl was more convinced than ever that she'd been left in the charge of someone not quite right in the head. "She's cruel, that's what she is."

But to Caroline herself she said, "Okay. Don't worry. You go now. Everything will be done before they come home."

"And don't forget to give them this letter," Caroline handed her a sealed envelope. "It has my phone number."

Rosie shrieked inwardly but spoke calmly, "Okay. There's a horn beeping. I think it's your taxi. You'd better go."

"You're very eager for me to leave. You're not up to anything, are you?"

Rosie looked hurt, "What would I be up to? I just don't want you to miss your train. I know you're dying to go on holiday."

Caroline softened, "I hope you don't think I want to be rid of you, Rosie, just because we didn't always get on."

Was she never going to leave?

"Why would I think that? There's that beeping again. The taxi-driver must be getting impatient. You'd better go. Have a lovely time." And she almost pushed the childminder out the door.

At last.

Looking at the sealed envelope, Rosie fought with her conscience. She should of course leave it for her parents. But what if the letter made it clear that Rosie wasn't going to Connemara? Yet if her parents ever found out she hadn't given them the letter, she'd be dead . . . well, perhaps they *would* be able to read it . . . if it didn't say anything too awful . . . Rosie held the envelope over the spout of the boiling kettle until the flap peeled back easily. She took out the page and read:

13th July

Dear Mr and Mrs McGrath,

Just to let you know, your daughter Rosie behaved very well during our week here. I know she thought I was a bit strict but she didn't really complain much. She did everything I asked, even coming with me to see antiques, which I know she found very boring.

My mobile phone number is 088-7634219. If you want to ask me anything, don't hesitate to ring.

I hope you had a good time in Paris and that it wasn't all hard work.

Rosie has insisted she'll be fine at home on her own and says she has cleared it with you and it's only for a few hours anyway.

All the best,

Yours sincerely,

Caroline.

Oh God! Why did Caroline have to put in that last sentence? Why did she have to give her phone number? Without those the letter was perfect. She could not show it to her parents – yet if she destroyed it and they ever found out, she'd be in desperate trouble. Rosie read it over and over. Desperate, she began to scrunch the page when she had a brainwave. Closely, she read again. Yes! It might work. It would have to. All she needed was a black ballpoint and she found one in the drawer.

She blackened out the word *at* and over it she put *going*, copying Caroline's writing, so that now the last sentence read:

Rosie has insisted she'll be fine going home on her own and says she has cleared this with you and it's only for a few hours anyway.

Yes!

And by changing 3 to 8 in the phone number, she made sure her parents couldn't contact Caroline.

Then, feeling more than a bit sneaky, she reminded herself that this was all in a good cause and she wouldn't have had to change the letter if she could've told her parents the truth. But that was impossible.

She stuck down the envelope with Pritt Stick and left it on the mantelpiece. Of course, if the childminder ever rang her parents, Rosie would be dead. But there was no point worrying about that.

She filled her huge rucksack with things from the kitchen. Then, at the back of the cupboard she noticed a litre bottle of gin. It was very dusty. "Mum and Dad mustn't want it," she reasoned. "It must be here ages. They'll never miss it." She added the gin to her store. Then, folding the old newspaper carefully, she put it into the front pocket.

At the shops she bought three chocolate oranges and a twelve-pack of cheese and onion crisps, some sweets, and a dozen fun-sized Coke. She'd never met anyone in the past who'd disliked Coke. Packing it all in, she staggered off.

It was less than a fifteen-minute walk to her destination. On the way down the hill to Drumcondra she passed the High Park Laundry, the school and the Crofton Hotel, wondering what changes she'd see in 1943. At the police station she turned right and made her way past Corpus Christi church until at last she was standing outside number 35 Griffith Avenue.

It was a pleasant house, set back from a long garden, with steps up to the front door and roller blinds half-drawn in the bay windows. As she looked, it occurred to Rosie that maybe some of the O'Neill family still lived there. Not Edward though. She swallowed. If Edward had escaped execution he couldn't possibly be still alive, not at 113 years of age! Rosie had heard of a lady in France who'd lived to be 127, but she was unique. All the same, the paper had mentioned Edward's son, Patrick.

"Maybe he still lives here. If he does, then I can ask him

what happened. It'd be daft to go back in that case!" She felt vaguely disappointed, as if the prospect of a great adventure was being snatched away.

About to open the gate and make inquiries, she was saved the trouble by a boy's appearance at the front door. He was on his way out and asked, "Are you looking for someone?"

"Does Mr O'Neill live here?" Rosie said.

"Never heard of him. We're Thompsons."

"Oh. Have your family lived here long?"

"Ages. Since before my older brother was born and he's twenty now. There's no one called O'Neill living around here." He swung out the gate past her and waved as she thanked him.

She looked around. On the opposite side of the road, a woman was walking her dog. Some distance away, at a bus stop, a few teenagers were trick-acting and farther down a couple of joggers were disappearing in the distance. She saw the boy turn into a house, probably calling for a pal. No one noticed her. The afternoon traffic was quiet, though she could hear the rumble of lorries on the main road. The avenue of trees swayed in the summer breeze.

Taking the photograph from her rucksack, Rosie concentrated on Edward's face. She heard the front door open, but when she glanced up there was no one there. Her imagination was working overtime, she thought.

"Maybe this is not going to work." But then the journey back had never been that easy. "Let me think. I have to do everything properly, step by step." It struck her then. "The watch. I'm stupid."

Swiftly she changed the year on her watch to 1943. Taking the newspaper from the rucksack she held it with the photograph and concentrated a minute on both. Her mind full of his image, she silently called, 'Edward!' There was a sudden dazzle of light across the bay windows of the house and she clearly saw the figure of a man looking at her, his hand half-raised as if in greeting. Then the light changed and the figure was gone.

Desperately, she looked at the photo, then at the report in the paper. Disjointed words echoed in her mind. *Businessman. Edward O'Neill. Arrested.* She closed her eyes and the words came faster: *Remains found. Murder suspect. Arguments. Motive. Edward O'Neill. Handcuffs.* Words repeated themselves and shouted in her brain: *Edward O'Neill! Murder suspect! O'Neill! Murder! Edward O'Neill! Edward O'Neill!* His name screeched in her head.

Suddenly there was silence. Nothing. Not the distant sound of traffic, nor the shouts of teenagers nor the bark of a dog. The leaves stopped whispering. Absolute silence. And in that moment Rosie felt a change in the atmosphere around her as time slipped. The trees, which had seemed to hold their breath, now rustled to a different breeze. A horse and cart went by. She could hear someone whistling and the sound of children at play.

Rosie opened her eyes. The newspaper print blurred. She tried to fold the sheets but they suddenly crumpled and flaked, becoming dust at her feet. The glass of the photograph glinted and for a second she thought Edward was smiling, but it was a trick of the sunlight. Then, as she reached down to her rucksack, she saw something else which was no illusion.

"Oh my God!" Disgusted, she noted the shiny black shoes she was wearing, with their thin crossover straps and small

25

heels. Worse still were her neatly turned-down short white socks. She groaned. Then she noticed her dress. "*Aagh*," she wailed. "This is *so* horrible!" It was red and white check, with a full skirt and some sort of white elastic stitching across the chest. To top it off, she had a knitted white cardigan with red and white check buttons. "Check buttons!" she moaned. "Gross! This is the worst I've ever had to wear." She fingered the offending buttons and realized they'd been covered in the same material as her dress. "I'm all matching and tidy. It's awful! This is so bad! It's worse than 1920."

She remembered almost with fondness the man's jacket she'd worn then, over the scratchy woollen dress and dirty apron. They might have been truly horrible but at least they hadn't been prim and prissy and, and – she struggled for the right word – and *neat!* Then she caught a movement at the window. Her eyes narrowed but she could not see behind the net curtains. A moment later the door opened and shut. It was the sound she'd heard some minutes before. It had happened too early then, like the appearance of the man at the window. They were small incidents that were required to wait and start again, when time had slotted into place and events were ready to unfold.

Rosie noticed the door was no longer blue, but dark green. The garden had changed too, had different flowers and plants and less lawn.

A man came striding down the path, his tweed jacket swinging. As he passed Rosie he raised his hat and smiled.

For a minute she was paralysed, blinking in the sunlight. Then she gathered her wits and clutching the photograph and rucksack, ran after him, shouting, "*Edward! Edward!*"

Chapter 4

The tall man ahead of her was lost in thought and did not hear. But the fellow she'd heard whistling did. He had been standing at the side of his cart, pouring milk from a tin measure into a jug when he'd heard Rosie's shouts. "You're a very cheeky young one," he said severely.

"What do you mean?" Rosie paused.

"Calling Mr O'Neill *Edward*, that's what I mean. Very cheeky!"

"But that's his name!" Rosie was bewildered.

"It may well be," said the young man gravely, "but it's not for a young one like you to be calling him that. Even his next-door neighbours wouldn't do that. You shouldn't be so forward!" He took the pint of milk up to a house where a woman waited at the door. "Here you are, *Mrs Kennedy*," he called, making a point of the woman's name. "That'll be three pence."

Rosie flew after Edward. "*Mr O'Neill*," she yelled, "*Mr O'Neill, stop!*"

The tall man halted and turned. Rosie caught up with him. She stared at him. Except for the brown eyes he was

unrecognisable as the twelve-year-old she'd met in 1920.
But then 43 years had passed for him. Now he was a
distinguished-looking middle-aged man, slim, well-dressed
and, from what she could see under his hat, grey-haired. His
face was kind and a little thin, a hint of worry in its lines.
But the eyes still had a boyish quality, a hidden flicker of
mischief, only needing an opportunity to light up.

Waiting politely for the girl to recover her breath,
Edward looked at her quizzically. There was something
familiar about her . . . she reminded him of someone long
ago. Memory niggled. "Do I know you?" he asked.

"You do," she gasped.

"Are you one of Mrs Brennan's daughters? No, you can't
be; they're very small. Maybe you're a relation?" Mrs
Brennan had two daughters and Edward couldn't tell one
from the other. They looked pale and peaky as well as small,
not like the girl in front of him.

"I'm not!" she said, then teased, "You mightn't know me,
Edward, but I know you. The last time I met you, you lived
in Sandymount."

Taken aback by her use of his first name, he struggled for
recognition. But it was impossible, unless . . . "I haven't
lived in Sandymount for more than thirty years. You weren't
even born then . . ."

I'm not even born now, Rosie thought, but shrugged
away the unsettling notion. She smiled and his eyes
narrowed. "I'll give you some clues," she said. "You had a
cook who made semolina that tasted like cement. And you
planned Henry's rescue when Foley kidnapped him, and
then we were trapped in a fire and we went to see Queen
Victoria and –"

"*Rosie! You're Rosie!*" Edward shouted, startling the young milkman who'd drawn nearer on his house calls. He was even more startled to see Mr O'Neill seize the girl by the hands and do a little jig with her on the path.

"My goodness," Edward said when he'd calmed down, "I never expected to see you again! And now that I do see you, why you don't look very much older than all those years ago. You must have the secret of eternal youth, Rosie!"

"I know that for you it's a long time since we met, Edward, but it's only a few months for me."

He sighed, "I remember how excited Henry and I were by your stories. But, as we grew up, that week and everything that happened then began to seem unreal, like a fairytale belonging to childhood. And since we could never explain those events in a way that made sense, we stopped talking about them. But I never forgot you, Rosie, though you've just given me a terrible shock." He was silent for a moment, swallowing. "You have no idea what it's like to have you turn up from my childhood, just as you were then. It's like being visited by a ghost."

"Well, I'm not a ghost!" Rosie was all the more firm because Edward's words spooked her. "And I'm not exactly the same. My clothes are different for a start."

He laughed. "Yes, they are. And your hair. Somehow I'd never have imagined you with curls."

"Curls!" There was nothing ghostly about Rosie's disgust as she put a hand to her hair and felt a mass of ringlets. "Oh no! Sausage curls! This isn't my hair. I have straight hair!"

"Not now, you haven't. They're very nice, Rosie. You look angelic."

The angel glared at him and his grin reminded her again

of the boy he'd been. Then he became serious. "I'm delighted you're here, Rosie. If you're going to stay, and I hope you are, we'd better sort out a few details. I finished work early and was on my way for an afternoon stroll, but I think we'd better go back and I'll introduce you to the family."

"Best leave the talking to me," Edward murmured as he turned the key in the hall door. He ushered her down the hall and into the dining-room. Rosie saw a boy about her own age, seated at a table, building something from pieces of metal. A woman sat in an armchair sewing a patch onto a pair of tweed shorts. She turned and the boy jumped up as they entered.

"This is Rosie," Edward said, frowning with the effort of thinking up a plausible story. But before he could say anything further, his son exclaimed, "Dad said we might be having a girl to stay. You must be her." He sounded disappointed. "You look very much like a girl. I hope you're not going to be boring and prissy."

While Rosie was digesting his words, Mrs O'Neill said quickly, "Patrick, don't be so rude! Of course she looks like a girl! What were you expecting Mr Hammond's daughter to look like?"

"Ah, yes, Mr Hammond's daughter – indeed," Edward said and then added as if for his son's benefit, "You remember Mr. Hammond, the company manager?"

"Of course he remembers!" his wife was impatient. "A pity your memory isn't as good, Edward. Why didn't you tell us Rosie was arriving today?" She turned to the girl. "I do hope your mother's operation is successful. Now, I know you wanted to stay at home with your father, but it's a trying time for the poor man. He'll be in and out to the hospital which is no place for a young girl and that's why I told Edward to say you'd be very welcome here."

She smiled and Rosie managed, "Thank you very much."

Mrs O'Neill turned on her husband again. "You can be very vague, Edward. We could have given Rosie a better welcome if we'd known she was coming today. Why on earth didn't you say something?"

"Eh . . . it was a surprise . . . for young Patrick, I mean."

Patrick was not impressed. "I'd prefer if she were a boy," he said. "Then she could play football and climb trees and things. She's too neat and tidy. Look at her curls!"

Before his mother could object again, Rosie answered for herself, "I am not neat and tidy. I was never neat and tidy!"

Mrs O'Neill groaned inwardly.

"And I don't like my curls! They weren't my choice. Anyway, you should look at your own hair before criticising other people's!"

"My hair? There's nothing wrong with my hair. It's not like a set of tubes! It's good, my hair is!"

"It looks like a greasy pancake!" Rosie was blunt. "And it's plastered onto your head!"

"That's not grease, it's haircream and I'd rather have a pancake than fat sausages!"

He glared at her and his father said, "Now, now! I hoped the two of you were going to be friends."

Mrs O'Neill added, "Rosie is our guest, Patrick. You shouldn't insult her." Privately she thought that now the girl had said so, her son's hair did resemble a pancake. She must get him to stop using that greasy stuff.

Patrick looked both ashamed and indignant. He supposed he had been very rude. He'd not met many girls so far, except for the Brennan sisters and they were all prim and proper and whingey. This one looked the part, but she was in no way whingey. In fact she was ready to fight back even though she was among strangers. Maybe he'd got it wrong.

"Sorry," he muttered.

She startled him by saying, "So am I. And your hair is better than mine. I hate mine." They looked at each other and grinned.

Edward and his wife were relieved. Patrick could be a right pain when he didn't like someone. He never hid his feelings and he could make the girl's stay a misery, though she seemed well able to look after herself.

"Let's start again," Edward said. "Rosie, this is my wife, Maria, and that boy there with the beautiful hair is my son Patrick. Now that you're formally introduced, you're very welcome – isn't she, Patrick?"

"Yes, Dad." He smiled at Rosie.

A few minutes later, Rosie almost lost his goodwill again.

She was sipping the glass of milk Maria had given her and was looking at the metal structure Patrick had been building. "That looks like a tin box with holes in it," she told him and hoped she sounded interested.

He drew himself up. "That is a car," he said curtly.

"A car?" Rosie sniggered. She hadn't seen a 1943 car yet, but it couldn't look like that.

"Well, of course a girl wouldn't appreciate Meccano!" His voice was hostile. "A girl wouldn't be interested in building cranes and cars and bridges!"

Not if they all look like tin boxes with holes, Rosie

wanted to say, but instead told him, "Don't start all that about girls again. I've never seen Mec – whatever – before and I just wondered what it was and how it worked."

Patrick struggled between amazement at such ignorance and the desire to show Rosie the wonders of his Meccano set. To his parents' huge relief he settled for the latter and sat down beside her, opening out the plans. Soon the two were engrossed. While Patrick put the wheels on his car, Rosie constructed a small crane, delighted she could follow the plans.

"This is cool," she told him, then seeing his puzzlement added, "I mean neat, really brilliant. Great." Not for the first time she wondered why words had to change their meanings over the years.

"You're very good at it. For a –" Patrick closed his mouth, catching Rosie's look.

As he put the last touches to the car, she looked around the room. The wallpaper was dark green, matching the lino on the floor and in the hall. A large mirror hung over the mahogany mantelpiece with lots of china ornaments. In one alcove was a huge old-fashioned valve radio. In the other were bookshelves. A large vase of flowers stood on a majestic oak sideboard, which matched the oak table and chairs. On either side of the fireplace was a small armchair. Although it was a sunny afternoon, the room looked quite gloomy.

In the alcove, over the radio, hung a large photo. Rosie caught her breath. It was the same as the one she'd brought with her, only bigger. "Joseph and Louisa," she murmured, "and Edward and Henry."

Since Mrs O'Neill was in the kitchen and Edward was

putting Rosie's rucksack into the spare room, it was only Patrick who heard her. His eyes followed hers. "How do you know their names?" he asked.

Rosie stared at him. The doorbell saved an answer.

Mrs O'Neill emerged from the kitchen. "Patrick!"

The boy rose reluctantly, looked keenly at Rosie and went to open the door. A female voice followed him back down the hall and a large woman with an apron over her dress came in excitedly.

"Mrs O'Neill, Mrs O'Neill! Let young Patrick get down to *Pay an' Take* immediately, for I believe there's a big consignment of flakemeal after coming in and the queue is already a mile long." The large woman stopped to breathe.

"Thanks for telling me, Mrs Kennedy. By the way, that's Rosie Hammond. She's staying with us while her mother's in hospital."

"Aw! And hasn't she lovely curls! I hope you enjoy your wee stay, Rosie. And isn't it lucky you're here? For you can take my ration card and get me some flakemeal. You'll save my tired legs a lot of trouble. Will you do that, Rosie? You with the lovely curls?"

Rosie felt like kicking Mrs Kennedy and said, rather ungraciously, "Why can't Patrick get your message as well as his mother's?"

"Dear Lord, where have you been living? As everybody knows, love, they'll only allow so much for each customer. Surely you wouldn't miss the opportunity for a wee walk with Patrick there. You'll have to tell me how you get your hair like that. I'd like to try it myself."

Astounded, Rosie tried to imagine sausage ringlets on the large woman's head.

"Mrs Kennedy does home perms," Maria explained.

Patrick threw fuel on the fire. "Maybe she could give you a home perm, Rosie, when your ringlets grow out. It only takes five hours and then you'd have your magnificent mop back again." He smirked.

However, his face changed when Mrs Kennedy cackled, "Oh ho ho! Well now, hasn't he got an eye for the girls! Oh, you'll want to keep an eye on that fellow, Mrs O'Neill, and him not out of short trousers yet!" And she roared laughing.

Rosie's face had gone dark with fury and Patrick's was a match. Looking at them, Maria expected an explosion any second and hastily gave Patrick some money. "Now, take the ration card and buy whatever you can get."

Mrs Kennedy handed a ten-shilling note and a card to Rosie and winked at her. "No doubt you're delighted to have a fine young fellow like Patrick taking an interest in you," she laughed, "but I'm not at all surprised, for it's seldom I've seen anyone with such shiny springy ringlets."

Rosie felt cursed. "You started all this!" she whispered to Patrick. "You're dead!"

"It's not my fault you've got curls," he snapped, raging that anyone would think he liked girls. Not that Rosie was bad-looking. Her hair might be ridiculous but she had a nice face. Yet if it weren't for her, Mrs Kennedy wouldn't have drawn attention to his short trousers. If he had proper parents he'd be in long trousers by now. After all, if a fellow was tall enough – and he was – why did he have to wait till he was fourteen before getting his first pair of manly trousers? And if a fellow didn't have longers, then he didn't need any silly girl drawing attention to the fact.

Rosie narrowed her eyes and considered strangling

Patrick, but just then Mrs Kennedy asked her, "And how long will you be staying, Rosie?"

"About a week," Rosie said.

Patrick groaned.

'Well, I just hope we all survive,' his mother thought and hurried them both out before Mrs Kennedy could mention curls again, or short trousers.

Chapter 5

They didn't speak on their way to the shop, each brooding on what a big pain the other was. Rosie sneaked a look at her companion. He wore striped braces over a short-sleeved shirt and corduroy shorts to his knees, which were scratched and scabby. His woolly socks were pushed down to his ankles and he wore sturdy lace-up boots. On his head was a school cap, pushed back from his forehead.

She noticed that most men wore a hat, even those on bikes. And she had never seen so many cyclists. They went whizzing down the hill in their hundreds. There were plenty of passengers too, mostly children who sat on crossbar saddles or on wicker seats at the back, their feet on metal footrests.

At first the only motor she saw was the number 3 bus trundling by. It had no automatic doors, just an open space at the back. She saw a boy jump off between stops and another race after the bus, weaving between bicycles, to be hauled on board by the conductor.

It was the horse traffic that fascinated her. Horse-drawn milk vans and bread vans. Carts stocked with goods. Carts carrying people. Carts of all sizes. But where were the cars? If there were buses, there had to be cars. She was about to ask Patrick when she saw a black one go by – with what looked like a hot-air balloon on the back. Her mouth dropped open. "What *is* that?" she said.

"Are you kidding me?" Patrick was scornful. "It's a car."

"I know it's a car. But what's that balloon thing at the boot."

He sighed, "It's for the gas that makes the car go. Fuel." He grew sarcastic. "Of course, you probably don't know there's a war on and –"

"Yes, I do. I know about the Emergency."

"Then you must know there's hardly any petrol and only doctors and suchlike have cars and they have to use gas."

"Right."

"And only a person who isn't normal wouldn't know about the gas balloons!"

"Oh, shut up," Rosie told him. Then her attention was distracted by something else. "Look at that queue. It's miles long!"

Patrick groaned. "I hate queuing. It's boring."

They joined the line of people and Patrick asked the woman in front, "Have you been waiting long?"

"A half an hour, son. But it'll be worth it to get a bit of flakemeal."

Rosie had never heard of flakemeal. Now she imagined some exotic food, a meal of chocolate flakes maybe. After all, it must be something delicious to make people join such a long queue. "What's flakemeal?" she asked Patrick.

Astonished, he looked at her. She was serious. "It's for

38

making porridge," he said, "or you can use it to bake brown bread. Don't you know *anything*?"

"I know I don't like porridge. Or brown bread." Rosie was glum.

"I love porridge, especially with the top of the bottle on it." Patrick's eyes lit up. "And the brown bread Mother makes is much nicer than that dark old shop bread."

Rosie's mum had recently decided to try out different breads. 'We have to be more adventurous,' she'd said. 'There's more to life than the sliced pan.' So now Rosie said rather grumpily, "But brown bread is not nicer than Vienna roll, or baguettes, or croissants, or pitta or pannini or foccacia –" She stopped, suddenly catching Patrick's expression.

"Pitta, pannini," he mimicked. "Never heard of them." He grew mock-serious. "They're foreign words. Are you a foreigner, Rosie? Maybe you're Italian. An Italian spy!"

"Don't be silly!"

Catching the note of worry, Patrick said gravely, "You could be arrested. Then you'd be interned in the Curragh. You'd be famous – the only child spy in the country – in Europe – in the world!"

"I am not a spy!" Rosie insisted.

"Then how do you know all those foreign names? Besides, it'd explain a lot if you were a spy."

"But I'm not. And what do you mean, 'explain a lot'?"

"It would explain why you're so strange, why you don't know about things here, like gas balloons and flakemeal. It isn't because you're not normal; it's because you're a spy!"

Patrick was beginning to convince himself. He considered. "I know you're a girl," he said. "And I know girls are not the same as boys –"

"It doesn't take a genius to work that out," Rosie snapped, "but being a girl doesn't make me a spy."

"I was going to say that even girls know about Meccano and gas balloons!"

"And so do I!" She stretched the truth. To distract him, she added, "I know more about them than you know about girls. You know nothing about girls!"

"I do so. I know they're telltales and teacher's pets and only want to play with dolls and won't get their frocks dirty and never get into trouble and never have adventures and they don't play football or climb trees or rob apples or do anything!"

"Oh, they don't, don't they? Well, they do, so they do!"

"No, they don't, so they don't. They definitely don't! "

"No, they don't though."

"Yes, they do though, so they do! Or do they? No, they don't! Definitely, they don't. You're trying to mix me up!"

They stopped. It was like a chorus in a mad song, Rosie thought, and they had taken each other's lines.

"How many girls do you know?" she asked.

"None. I don't have anything to do with girls."

"Are there girls in your class?"

"Don't be daft! Do I look as if I go to a girls' school? I'm in the Christian Brothers."

"You could be in a mixed school," Rosie told him.

"No, I couldn't. There aren't any mixed schools – not after you're seven."

"But you must talk to girls? At least sometimes?"

"Not unless I have to. Sometimes I have to talk to the Brennan girls. That's if I'm with Ma. But I only say hello, 'cos they're a pain. They cry if they get mud on their shoes and if you borrow their ball they're straight in to tell their da. And they're always playing with their dolls – they have about ten dolls sitting in their prams and they spend all day talking to them or changing their clothes! They're no fun."

"They sound miserable," Rosie said. "What age are they?"

Patrick shuffled a little and had the grace to redden. "Eh . . . about six," he muttered.

"Six!" Rosie was scornful. "Six! Ah, come on! The only girls you know are six years old. You mean, you hate all girls and you won't talk to them because the only ones you know are two little kids who like dolls and tell on you when you rob their ball!"

"Borrow, not rob." Embarrassed, he tried to defend himself by finding his companion's weak point. "Anyway, I bet *you* don't like boys. I bet you don't talk to them either!"

Rosie thought of the boys in her class at Collins' Community School and of David Byrne in particular. She had detested him at first because he seemed a bit of a show-off. But that was because he found it hard to sit still. He had megatons of energy and was always being corrected by teachers for running instead of walking, climbing over desks instead of going round them, swinging on his chair and talking non-stop during lessons.

But he had a wicked sense of humour, never ratted and was often generous. Rosie quite liked him now. And she wouldn't fancy school without boys. They liked different things maybe, like football and racing cars and they had different opinions, but that just made classes more interesting.

So now she told Patrick, "You're wrong. I do like boys.

41

Not all of them though." She glanced his way and he found himself wondering was it him she didn't like. Unreasonably, he felt disappointed, then annoyed at himself for wishing she liked him, so he said, "I don't want to talk about stupid things anyway. You changed the subject from spies and –"

"Oh, don't start all that again!" Rosie was fed up. "I'm not a spy, right!"

"Well, you're . . ." Patrick didn't want to repeat himself but he could find no different words, "You're not normal. You're strange."

"I'm strange? I'm not the one who puts the top of a bottle on his porridge!"

"Sorry?" He was distracted once more and struggled to understand. Then his brow cleared. "When I said the top of the bottle, I meant the cream at the top of the milk."

But she was no longer listening. Her attention had switched to a man and woman some way up the queue. Her eyes widened and she remembered her visit to 1956.

"It's them," she said. "It's Gran and Grandad!"

"What?" Patrick exclaimed. "Where are they? I thought you'd no relatives and that's why you're in our house. Where are your gran and grandad? Maybe you could stay with them."

Rosie was still staring at the couple, not listening. The man's hand rested on his wife's shoulder and, when she turned sideways, the girl could see she was holding a baby in a blanket.

That must be Uncle Jack, she thought. Mum isn't even born yet. They must be living in our house on Innish Road. I should say hello to them. I might never see Grandad again.

She was overcome with the desire to run up the queue

and talk to her grandfather. He had died before she was born. When she'd met him during her first trip to the past, Rosie had really liked him. She never thought she'd get the chance to see him again. Now she took off.

"Rosie, Rosie!" Why was that dratted girl racing up the line? Had she really seen her grandparents? What on earth was she doing now, talking to that young couple with the baby? Was he hearing properly? Had she called the man 'Grandad'? A man who was hardly old enough to be her father!

Patrick felt his face blaze. It was just his luck. No other fellow had a lunatic staying in his house.

He arrived at Rosie's side to hear the man say, quite kindly, "I think you've made a mistake, Miss. I'm not your grandfather. Give me a bit more time. I'm only new to the fathering business. Got a long way to go before this little fellow makes me a grandad."

His wife smiled and the man behind them in the queue said, "I think the young lady must be joking, Mr O'Brien, though I can't see exactly where the laugh is."

O'Brien! She was right. They *were* her grandparents. A number of people were looking curiously at her and, with Patrick tugging at her sleeve, she realised there was nothing she could do. She could not enter her grandfather's world. It wasn't what she'd come back for.

"I'm sorry," she said, "I made a mistake. I haven't seen my grandad for a while. You reminded me of him."

"You must have the youngest granpa on earth," said the man behind, his tone mocking.

"Don't mind him," said Mr O'Brien. "It's just a case of mistaken identity. You must miss him a lot?"

Rosie nodded, grateful for his kindness. "I didn't think I did, but I do," she said.

Patrick wasn't a bit sympathetic, "You're daft," he told her, "running up to a stranger and calling him 'Grandad'. Now you've lost us our place in the queue and it's longer than ever. Mother will be so disappointed if the flakemeal is all gone. And we'll never hear the end of it from Mrs Kennedy." She'd probably go on about how he'd been too distracted by Rosie to bother about the message. She wouldn't let the matter rest for years.

It was Rosie's grandmother who came to the rescue. She had seen the strain on the girl's face and the boy's glum expression. Glancing around her, she noted everyone was chatting, no longer looking at the girl. She made some space. "Nip in here, in front of me, before anyone notices," she told them. Patrick pushed Rosie into the queue, beaming at Mrs O'Brien.

Her grandad was chatting away now to the man behind about football. Patrick joined in while her gran listened.

She looked at the baby. He was smiling at her. "Hello, Jack," she said and tickled his chin. The baby's face changed and he began to cry.

Her gran turned, soothing him. "How do you know his name?"

Rosie shrugged, "You must have said it."

"I don't think so." Something about the girl puzzled Mrs O'Brien. The mistake she'd made was very odd. Had she seen her before? She reminds me of someone, she thought. But she did not connect Rosie with the girl she'd met in the past. How could she? Yet the sense of familiarity nagged her.

"Do I know you?" she asked.

The girl blushed. She wondered what would happen if she explained, "You're my gran and when I get back to my own time you'll be ninety-three years of age. But I've met you twice before on my journeys to the past: once with granda in 1956 (only you can't remember that because it hasn't happened to you yet) and once in 1920."

Sighing, Rosie knew there was no point. Shifting uncomfortably under her gran's keen stare, she did not answer but focused her attention on the baby. "Who's a lovely boy?" she said.

The lovely boy wasn't at all charmed. He screwed up his face, turned a furious red and started bawling, tears falling in big drops.

"You have a way with infants," Patrick said, then cried, "*Ouch*! You kicked me. That hurt!"

"Sorry," Rosie smiled with false sympathy. Her gran was still looking at her.

All the time the queue had been moving. A sudden surge brought them inside the shop and Mrs O'Brien turned to the business in hand, forgetting about the girl.

"Two pounds of flakemeal for each customer," said one of the assistants. "That's two and nine pence and one coupon."

Deftly the woman scooped the flakemeal from a huge sack into a brown-paper bag, folded it down twisting the corners and exchanged it for Rosie's ten-shilling note and a coupon from the ration card. The till made a loud ringing noise and crashed open. "Seven and thruppence." She handed Rosie her change.

As the girl waited for Patrick, she noticed other sacks filled with sugar and dark flour on the floor behind the mahogany counter. Farther along on the inside counter was a marble top on which rested slabs of butter and wheels of Cheddar cheese. The shelves behind held glass jars and bottles, some of them tiny, in all kind of different colours. But the shop was only half-stocked, with plenty of space on the shelves.

Her gran had got her flakemeal and the assistant took her order for butter and cheese. Rosie watched fascinated as the woman lifted two wooden clappers from a bowl of water to cut and shape a square of butter, before returning them to the water. She wrapped and weighed the butter, then turned her attention to a wheel of cheese, deftly slicing a triangle with a wire.

She could have watched for ages, but Patrick was tugging at her. "Come on, Rosie! You're holding up the queue."

Rosie! Her gran turned from the counter. *Rosie.* Where had she heard that name before? Childhood memories tugged and she saw the hazy image of a girl from long ago, Someone she'd known only briefly. When exactly was it? She concentrated. A face flashed into her mind. The same face as this girl's! Now she knew her. They'd met during that awful week in 1920!

Rosie saw the sudden shock of recognition and, as her gran began to speak, she turned on her heel and hurried from the shop.

Mrs O'Brien was about to follow when the assistant called, "Hey, Missus! Don't forget your flakemeal!"

She stopped and common sense returned. It wasn't possible this girl could be the same one she'd met nineteen years ago. How could she have thought so, even for a second? She must be overtired, what with the baby and the warm weather. She'd best have a lie-down as soon as they got home. Imagine fancying she'd met someone from her childhood – someone who had hardly got any older. Daft!

Chapter 6

'Gran looked really shocked when she heard my name,' Rosie thought as they went home. 'Did she remember where she met me?' She sighed. 'I wish I could have said a proper goodbye to Grandad, but I couldn't hang around. Pity I can't visit him.' She sensed that she could not go out of her way to see her grandfather, that since she had come back for one reason – to help Edward – she must concentrate on this, otherwise things could go badly wrong.

Thinking about what might have been preoccupied her all the way home.

Patrick too was silent, wondering was he right about girls and deciding this particular one wasn't like *anyone* he'd met before. For a start, there were the things she didn't know that every other person knew. Then there were the things she did know, like foreign words.

And she could argue. She didn't burst out crying like those Brennan twins when he'd asked them to give him one good reason why he couldn't borrow their ball. He hadn't even wanted their stupid ball, just politely wondered why they wouldn't lend it. Then their da had come out and said he was a bully and to pick on someone his own size or he, Mr Brennan, would pick on him with a clip around the ear. And all he'd done was ask!

At least Rosie wasn't a whinger. But she *was* strange. Look how she'd behaved with that couple. No one in their right mind could have mistaken them for grandparents. But it wasn't just a mistake. The way Mrs O'Brien had asked if they had ever met! And when she'd heard Rosie's name she'd looked shocked first, then grey and then sick, as if she'd seen a ghost.

Not many people he knew had that effect on others, Patrick thought. Why on earth had she run up that line and called that man Grandad? He had to ask and when he did Rosie had her answer ready.

"That queue was very long," she said, "and Mrs O'Brien had a kind face."

"You mean . . ." He couldn't believe it. "You mean you were trying to skip the queue?"

She smiled.

"You have a nerve," he said, more admiring than critical. "You could've got into terrible trouble. There are shocking fights over queue-skippers."

She said nothing and Patrick suddenly cheered up. It occurred to him that Rosie was going to be a lot more interesting than he'd first believed.

Mrs Kennedy was delighted with her flakemeal and gave them each a penny. "Don't spend it all in the one shop," she joked, then winked at Patrick. "Of course you'll probably buy something nice for wee Rosie here, amn't I right now?"

Patrick blushed and mumbled and when they'd gone down the path, he said with fury, "I hate her!"

Rosie didn't answer, still taken aback at being given the huge sum of one penny.

Patrick's mother had tea ready when they arrived home and Rosie sat down expectantly. She was quite hungry. Mrs O'Brien put a plate of bread on the table. It was very odd-looking. It wasn't brown bread but it wasn't white either.

This was followed by some butter, a bowl of mashed bananas and a teapot.

Maria poured some very watery tea. Rosie watched Edward butter his bread and spread the slice with banana. She followed suit and took a bite. Closing her eyes in shock, she swallowed quickly and, meeting Maria's eyes, managed to smile.

"It's very like banana, isn't it? Do you like it, Rosie?" Maria was quite proud of the mix.

It's revolting, the girl wanted to tell her. I've never tasted anything so horrible. Instead she asked, "What exactly is it?"

"Mashed parsnips and banana essence. The recipe was given on the radio. It's like the real thing, isn't it?"

Rosie looked at Patrick and Edward. They were munching away. "How long is it since you've eaten real bananas?" she said.

The boy stared at her but Edward said hastily, "The last one I had was in 1939."

Four years ago. They must have completely forgotten the taste if they thought mashed parsnip was similar.

"Do you not like them?" Maria was anxious. "I thought they'd be a treat, seeing as the tea is so weak. We're running

49

low and I've used those tea leaves twice already, so I thought at least the bananas –"

"The bananas are very unusual." Rosie tried to make this sound like a compliment. "I've never tasted anything like them before. My mother mustn't have heard of that recipe." Thank heavens, she added silently, while Maria smiled with relief.

Anyway, Rosie thought, why was she eating this awful stuff when she had real bananas in her rucksack? Abruptly she pushed back her chair, excused herself and left the room.

"I hope she's not unwell," Maria said.

"She's not normal. That's definite." Patrick was still puzzling over Rosie's ignorance regarding bananas. Everyone in the whole world knew bananas had stopped arriving with the war. Except Rosie, it seemed.

"Maybe I should see if there's anything wrong?" Edward said, but at that moment Rosie arrived back in the room with a large bunch of bananas.

Maria's mouth dropped and Patrick nearly fell off the chair in his effort to touch them. They were real!

"Where on earth did you get these?" Maria lifted the bunch from the table and looked at them from every angle. "They're beautiful," she murmured. "But it's not possible – how did – ?"

Edward cut in, "Maria, you're embarrassing the girl. You should never ask anyone how they get anything on the black market. I know her father has a lot of connections, but that's none of our business." This was rubbish, he knew. Nobody, *nobody*, could import bananas. The seas were too dangerous because of the war. His wife knew this too, he was aware. "Let's just enjoy them," he said, "and not ask any questions."

Maria was amazed. Her husband had never approved of the black market before. And seeing she was not about to be diverted, he broke off a banana and peeled it. Then he put a piece in his mouth and his eyes grew large with pleasure. "This is wonderful!" he exclaimed. "This is the best! This is only –"

"A banana," Rosie finished, thinking Edward had lost his senses. It was only a bit of fruit, after all, quite nice, but not something to die for.

Maria could not bear it. Forgetting any misgivings, she took one, peeled it and took a bite. Her eyes closed. "This is exquisite!" she moaned. "This is definitely not mashed parsnip!"

Patrick could wait no longer. His banana lasted three seconds. After the first bite, he stuffed in the rest, cheeks bulging.

"What do you think?" Rosie asked.

"Snicethingevtashtd," Patrick told her, his mouth full.

"What did you say?"

He waited till the last morsel was swallowed, then sat back, satisfied. "I said that was the nicest thing I ever tasted. It was yummy! How many have we left?"

"Three," said his mother. She looked at Rosie. "I don't care where you got them, but thank you very much for bringing them. Now we can't keep them all to ourselves! Patrick, I want you to take one in to Mrs Kennedy. She's a good neighbour. And I'll be visiting old Mrs Doyle tonight – I'm sure she'd love one. The last is for Rosie. She didn't have hers yet."

About to take one, Rosie changed her mind, unable to bear the three pairs of eyes looking at her with awful longing. "Actually, I don't really like bananas," she lied.

"My goodness!" Maria said. "In that case we might as well divide it between us. It might go off if we keep it till tomorrow." Rosie had never seen such enjoyment as they shared the last banana.

Patrick went next door with good enough grace, the precious fruit hidden in a brown-paper bag. He came back looking the worst for wear, his hair wonky and his face red, glaring at his mother.

"What's wrong?" Maria asked. "What happened? You look upset."

"I *am* upset," Patrick snarled. "When Mrs Kennedy opened the door I gave her the bag and told her it was a little present and to ask no questions. She said thanks very much, then looked in the bag and she – she – she screeched like a maniac. Then she did a little dance and threw her apron over her face."

"Well, it's not every day you see a banana," his father said. "She just got a bit over excited, that's all."

"It wasn't all! I said goodbye very quickly and was going when she got hold of me and gave me a big kiss and mussed my hair. She was hugging me and I couldn't breathe and lucky for me Mr Kennedy came to the door. But when he saw the banana I thought he was going to hug me too, so I ran." He slumped into a chair, totally depressed.

"Your hair looks better now," Rosie said. It was like fork-lightning, but Patrick didn't know that and he cheered up a little.

"Let's see!" He stood up to look in the mirror, then

wailed and turned on Rosie, "Oh, very funny! It looks mad."

"It suits you!" Rosie kept her face straight and his mother and father hid their smiles. Patrick rushed from the room and when he came back, his hair was wet, the grease washed out.

An hour later Maria took Patrick with her to see Mrs Doyle. The boy was a favourite of the old lady's and Patrick liked her. "But she'd better not kiss me when you give her that banana," he warned his mother.

"Let's listen to the War Commentary on the BBC," Edward said to Rosie, turning on the radio and twiddling the knobs till the static lessened.

The presenter announced in grave tones:

Today, Friday the 13th, saw more success for our troops in Sicily. The British and Canadian forces, led by Field Marshal Montgomery, are now only fifteen miles from Catania, the island's second largest city. And in North Africa the Allied advance is continuing without much serious resistance . . . In Europe the Allies have bombed military bases in Germany . . .

Rosie stopped listening, not wanting to follow a war that was over long before she was born.

Edward strained to hear every word and she remembered how interested he'd always been in battles. A few minutes later the reception went and the sound hissed and crackled. Edward turned off the radio.

"Now, Rosie," he turned to her, "tell me why you've come back."

Not wanting to worry him, she did not tell him the whole truth. "I wanted to see how you were. To find out what you and Henry were doing."

"Well, Henry is living in Switzerland. He's looking after the company's business there. You might remember Father started an import/export business, which we inherited. It's called *Donovan, O'Neill and Company*." He paused.

"Who's Donovan?" Rosie prompted.

"A partner in the company. A good man." He sighed. "He disappeared a year ago. Left work one Friday evening and didn't turn up on Monday. He lived on his own and drank, maybe out of loneliness." Edward stared into the distance, remembering. "Anyway, I thought he was sick and called to the house, but he wasn't there. After a couple of days when he hadn't come back I went to the police." He stopped again, his face sad. Then he continued, "They searched his house. All his clothes were in the wardrobe. As far as they could see, nothing was missing. They looked at his bank account, but he had no money, only borrowings. Anything he had, he spent on drink, as I told them."

"What do you believe happened to him?" Rosie asked.

"I dread to think. The best we can hope for is that he lost his memory and is out there somewhere. If he were dead – if an accident happened – then surely the police would have found his body."

Rosie remembered the newspaper report. "Did he ever take money from the company? For drink, maybe?"

"Not a penny. The police asked that too, apparently because of some rumour they'd heard. They wondered if we'd had a row over money, half-suggesting that I caused his disappearance. Well, if they think he ran off because of an argument with me, they're wrong!" He shuddered at the idea and was so upset that Rosie could not tell him the police would soon suspect him of much worse. "Michael is such a decent man," he sighed. "He never took a penny that didn't belong to him. He had no problems with drink when he joined the company and he had enough money then to buy a partnership. I don't know what went wrong and I wish now I'd asked him why he drank, but I didn't want to intrude, and drink didn't affect his work." He sighed again and Rosie sighed along with him, thinking of the near future and wondering how she was going to help.

Edward looked at her and said, "I shouldn't be burdening you with my problems."

She shook her head. "Is your business doing well, Edward?" she asked.

"We make a living. And every month I set aside Michael's share, hoping he'll turn up. It's difficult to do well with the war going on. But Henry has turned his hand to banking in Switzerland, until things get better. And he manages to get money through every so often." He cheered up at the thought of his brother. "Do you know, he's married and has ten-year-old twin daughters. Imagine! Another set of twins."

"They run in the family," Rosie said, telling him about Mum and Aunt Rose.

But she did not tell him that Gran was living less than two miles away. She must stick to the purpose of her trip and did not want events to become more tangled than they already were by Edward paying Gran a visit.

Trying to solving a murder mystery was enough!

Chapter 7

Edward told her the details of his life. When the Great War came in 1914, he had joined up, fought in France for the British Army and become a captain. Henry had failed the medical because of an ear condition and had stayed at home.

"You know that my father, Joseph, always felt he owed something to Britain?" said Edward. "He said the British army gave him his chance to escape from being poor. He passed that feeling of loyalty on to us. I joined up for that reason and because my head was full of silly notions about war being a great adventure. It wasn't. It was horrible. Young fellows blown to pieces, or left lying wounded on the battlefield for hours until our chaps could rescue them. And some of them shouldn't have been allowed to join up. They weren't old enough. One lad in my battalion was fourteen – a year older than you, Rosie. He looked his age too and should never have been accepted, but the government didn't care. What matter if it was kids firing the guns as long as the guns got fired? The youngsters lied about their age to join the great adventure – great bloodbath more like – and they put their trust in generals, a lot of whom had no respect whatsoever for them. And what was it all for, hey? Because here we are again, worse than last time!"

Rosie listened, but could think of no response that would help.

"Anyway, when I got home," Edward told her, "everything had changed. Ireland was not the country it had been when Queen Victoria visited. People didn't want to stay British. We wanted to rule ourselves. Henry was full of it and I began to see it was possible. We could do it. Of course there were some very dark days, but it was exciting too. Especially when the British left and we were in charge of our own destiny. I can't explain what a marvellous feeling that was!"

"What about Joseph? How did he feel?"

"Disappointed. He'd always been proud to be part of the British Empire. But he recognised that more and more Irish people felt the opposite and there was nothing he could do to change events – though I think he believed until the day he died that Ireland would have been better off had we remained British."

"When did he die, Edward?"

"In 1923, one year after our mother. He was sixty-seven. It was quite sudden. He was very healthy, still took an interest in the business. Then in January he caught a cold. which became pneumonia and within a month he was dying."

The worst thing about time-travel, Rosie thought, was that people you got to know, got to grow really fond of, belonged not only to the past, but to death. Edward himself would not be alive in her own time. She might never see him again after this visit. And she'd miss him, just as she missed Joseph and Grandad and so many others.

Her journeys, which had seemed so exciting earlier in the day, took on a darker aspect. She was tired of missing people.

Seeing her sadness, Edward assured her, "My father didn't suffer, Rosie. He just grew very weary and then one morning he didn't wake up. His death was tranquil. He said life had given him many gifts and he had been very fortunate. He wouldn't have wanted you to be sad." When she said nothing, he went on, "We used to talk about you. He asked if we remembered the week you came back. As if there was any forgetting! Towards the end he got a bit mixed up. He seemed to think he'd gone back in time. And he talked about meeting you when he was boy. His tiredness made for confusion, I suppose. He drifted peacefully into death."

"He wasn't confused," Rosie said. "He did go back to the past, to find his own father." She told him Joseph's story and how she came to meet him in Oak Park when he was fourteen.

A long silence followed as Edward reflected. Then he asked, "What was my father like then?"

Rosie thought. "Serious," she recalled. "Very poor. He hadn't yet learned to read or write. But he wanted to get on and he was good at making friends. He was brave too and adventurous." She told him of Joseph's visit to her own time.

Edward took a deep breath. "No wonder he thought life had been good to him. He had such wonderful experiences! And he got through his ragged childhood to become quite a wealthy man."

They sat again in silence, each remembering Joseph.

The doorbell rang and, as Edward answered it, Rosie thought of Joseph's qualities. 'He was a good person,' she concluded.

"Come in, come in, Mr Reddin." Into the room Edward ushered a thin ferret-faced man who looked sharply at the young girl.

"I was hoping you'd be on your own, Mr O'Neill. I've got important business to discuss. And little girls have big ears. Some have ears that are too large for their own good." He was looking at Rosie's with such distaste that she touched them immediately, wondering if they had grown in the last few seconds.

"Oh, she won't say a word to a soul," Edward said. "Rosie, this gentleman is Leonard Reddin. He says he was a friend of my partner, Michael Donovan."

"My ears are normal," Rosie replied. She was fed up with people saying she wasn't normal. "And I'm not a little girl! I'm thirteen."

Leonard Reddin met her annoyance with such a hostile look that she was startled. Then, with some effort, his expression changed to one of oily friendliness. "My apologies," he told her. "Of course you're not a child. You're a young lady. And your ears, if I may say so, are like delicate petals."

Mentally Rosie reached for the vomit bag, instantly preferring huge ears to sick compliments. But she did not want to be ill-mannered in Edward's house and reluctantly she shook the hand Reddin extended and wondered why he was wearing gloves.

"I've got a skin disease," he explained. "Some infection

that makes my hands break out in small, yellow, pus-filled boils."

Edward looked sympathetic but Rosie almost gagged, wishing she'd never shaken his hand. Reddin leered at her discomfort.

"Now, Mr O'Neill, down to business. If you don't mind the young lady's presence, then neither do I, though the matter is a bit sensitive."

"How can I help, Mr Reddin?"

"It's like I was saying. Donovan was my friend and because of our friendship I loaned him one thousand pounds towards buying a partnership in your company. I've come to you 'cause I was never paid back, see. To be blunt, I want you to give me what I'm owed."

"I see." Edward was thoughtful. "I am a little puzzled, Mr Reddin. You say you and Michael were friends and it's true only a good friend would lend such an amount of money. Yet he never mentioned your name."

"I can't help that!" the man snapped, then recovered at once. "It's easily explained. At the beginning Donovan wouldn't have wanted you to think he was in debt. Later on he fell out with me because I wanted my money back. So he wouldn't have talked about me, would he? But now he's gone, you've got his share and I've got nothing and I reckon that ain't fair, so it ain't!"

Edward sat up straight and looked Reddin in the eye. The man glanced away. "I hope you're not accusing me of taking what belongs to Michael!" Edward's voice was cold. "I've put the salary Michael would have drawn into an account for him, Mr Reddin! In spite of the fact that the firm is not very profitable."

"You must take me for a fool!" Reddin snarled. "Not profitable? Everyone knows you can smuggle goods to the North for a huge profit – and to England, if you've got the nerve. So don't tell me you're not making money. And you get to keep Donovan's share too. Oh, you have a nice little set-up!"

Edward paled with anger. "We are not a gang of smugglers in my company, Mr Reddin. As you know any black-marketeering is against the law. I'm not a criminal and I don't want to lose my licence. Now if you've finished, I think it's time you went."

He stood up, but the other man didn't move.

"Hold your horses," said Reddin. "Calm down, can't you! I was perhaps a bit hasty. I apologise." His voice was oily again. He waited till Edward was once more seated. "I'm only asking for what's mine, nothing more. Donovan put my money into your business. Now I should like it back. That's reasonable, ain't it?"

"How do I know you're telling the truth?"

"Ah. Well . . ." Donovan reached into his pocket and extracted a letter. With clumsy fingers he took out a folded sheet of paper. Before he stuffed the envelope back in his pocket, Rosie had plenty of time to study the address: *23 Whitworth Road, Drumcondra.*

Edward opened the page and read:

You know I cannot yet return your one thousand pounds. Nor do I agree to give you instead my one third of Donovan, O'Neill and Co. I might be having problems and arguments in the company but nothing you say or do will make me give up my share. You will have to wait for your money till I can honourably withdraw profits from the business.

God knows I'd love to pay you off and stop your endless torment!

As you know, everything is recorded in my journal.

Yours etc.

Michael Donovan.

The note was scrawled in a hurry, with no greeting or date, but Edward recognised his partner's handwriting. "It seems you're right, Mr Reddin." He sighed. "I wish Michael had come to me for help, but he was a proud man."

"He wasn't too proud to borrow and not pay back," Reddin was sharp. "And he wasn't too proud to drink himself stupid with money that wasn't by rights his!"

"I wonder what made him drink," Edward murmured. He looked at Reddin. "He writes that you tormented him. What did he mean?"

"He means I asked for my money! The thoughts of paying his debts were what tormented him! You can see I'm owed. What are you going to do about it?"

Before he could answer, Rosie butted in. "Why have you waited so long to visit Edward? Why didn't you come looking for your money earlier?"

Annoyed, Reddin snapped, "What business is it of yours, Miss Big Ears?"

"Big ears is better than petals any day," Rosie muttered.

Reddin heard. "Petals huh! Bicycle petals! Get it? Petals, pedals?" He sniggered.

"That's a stupid joke," Rosie said.

"But an excellent question on your part, Rosie," said Edward. "Why don't you answer it, Mr Reddin?"

Reddin stopped smiling and for a second he looked even

more shifty. Then he shrugged. "I didn't come here before because I didn't want to trouble you. I thought Donovan had gone on a bender and he'd turn up one day. You'd be upset enough, Mr O'Neill, I thought, without having someone on your doorstep immediately after his disappearance, looking for a thousand quid." He grew more confident. "I stayed away out of the goodness of my heart, but a man can only wait so long. What do you say? Are you going to do the decent thing?"

Edward reflected, saying nothing, and Reddin was forced to continue.

"Tell you what, Mr O'Neill. I reckon you're what Donovan calls honourable. So I'll trust you. Keep that note. It's no good to me. Think about what he wrote and I reckon you'll come to see I've got right on my side."

Reddin rose. "I'll call again, shall I, when you've had time to study the ins and outs?"

Edward nodded, relieved at the man's departure. He needed time to reflect.

Then Reddin asked, a bit too casually, "By the way, do you know anything about this journal of Donovan's? A diary, perhaps? If he kept a record like he says, that would be even more proof of his debt."

"If Michael had such a journal, I never saw it."

"Mmm. Well, I don't believe there was one," Reddin said. He sounded relieved. As Edward accompanied him to the front door, he added, "Donovan was a fool, especially when he was drunk. It's just another of his silly tricks to pretend he wrote everything in a journal!"

"Michael had a lot of problems," Edward said, "but I wouldn't dismiss him as a fool. I'll think about all you've told me and if I believe you, Mr Reddin, you'll get your money,"

"You do that," Reddin's voice rose sharply. "You have a good think, Mr O. Then you make sure you come to the right decision. It would be in your interest."

In the dining-room, Rosie shivered. The man's voice was full of menace.

She heard the front door close.

Edward came back very agitated. "What a vile fellow! Poor Michael!" He slumped into a chair.

"Do you think he might have kept a diary?" Rosie asked, thinking such a find might help Edward.

"I don't know. He told me once he was keeping a journal, but he had a few drinks on him and said if I ever wanted to see it, I'd find it behind bars with the cat. There was no sense to him sometimes when he was like that."

"Did he have a cat?" Rosie asked.

"No, he didn't. And he certainly wouldn't have kept one behind bars. What am I going to do, Rosie? How do I know if Reddin is genuine? Was he really a friend of Michael's? And did he lend him that money? The note seems to show he did."

"Why don't you give the note to the police?" Rosie said. "They might find the answer."

Edward hesitated, then sighed. "In his note Michael mentions arguments and problems in the company. It's true we argued, but never about business, only about his drinking. I wanted him to stop for his own sake. They were only arguments in the sense that we disagreed over the harm he was doing to himself. There was never any shouting or bitterness. But the police might believe otherwise. They might think that's why he went away I don't want them to say I drove him off so I could grab his share of the business."

As they studied the page, they heard the front door open and Edward quickly put the note in his pocket. "Not a word to Maria," he said. "She worries enough about the business as it is. Promise?"

Rosie nodded.

Edward was right, she thought. The note could only cause trouble for him.

Chapter 8

"I have to talk to you, in private," Rosie whispered to Patrick as soon as she could. She thought he would make some smart remark, but he just nodded and said, "Later."

Patrick wanted to find out more about this stranger who brought the kind of food not even smugglers could find.

During the evening he'd thought a lot about Rosie. She could have sold those bananas for a small fortune if she'd wanted to. And where on earth did she get them? Not from Mr Hammond, her father, Patrick was certain. *Donovan O'Neill* would never employ someone who smuggled. The company – his father in particular – was proud of its reputation for not making money out of the hardship of war. Da had often made that point, which was why Patrick couldn't understand it when he'd said Mr Hammond's smuggling was his own business. Perhaps he'd wanted to protect Rosie from any more of his mother's questions. Which meant the girl had something to hide. If she had, he was going to find out!

Edward and Maria listened to the ten past ten evening news

and then to The Silver Star Ceili Band and a singer called Peig. Rosie yawned and excused herself, saying she was tired. Patrick followed suit.

"Just as well to get a good night's rest," Maria said. "We'll be working hard on the allotment tomorrow."

Patrick followed Rosie into the small back room. She sat on the edge of the bed while he settled himself cross-legged on the floor.

"I want to know what's going on!" he said.

"You're not going to believe me, but I've got to tell you, Patrick, because I need your help. Just hear me out, will you? Don't say a word till I've finished. Please?"

He nodded and Rosie began.

She told him about her own time and of her gift for time-travel. She told him how they were related and how she'd come to know his father and that when she'd read a report of Edward's arrest, she'd had to come back to help him.

True to his word, Patrick said nothing, but she could see he was finding belief impossible.

"I'm telling you the truth," she said.

"Where's the newspaper report you say you read?" Patrick said. "That would be proof."

"I haven't got it. It crumbled away. Don't you see! It hasn't yet been written, so of course it couldn't come back to before its time, if you know what I mean."

Patrick was unconvinced. Yet it was obvious that Rosie believed what she said. But it was such a strange tale! It couldn't be true, could it?

"I could ask Da about you," Patrick said.

"No, don't. He won't want you to know he lied about who I am. And he'll have to keep up the pretence with

Maria, because she'd never believe my story. Adults usually think time-travel is impossible. And he might not like keeping a secret from her, when you know what it is. He might feel mean."

Rosie saw he was still uncertain. Desperate to make him believe her, she went to her rucksack. "Look." She handed him Joseph's family photograph.

"It's the same as the one downstairs," he said. "Where did you get it?"

"Look at the inscription on the back, Patrick."

He turned the photo.

To Rosie.
  Something to remember from 1900.
  Fondest regards, Joseph.

Patrick's face paled. He could hardly take it in. Time-travel was something immense, awesome.

Rosie mistook his shock for disbelief. She lifted the rucksack onto the bed and emptied its contents as further proof.

Now Patrick was even more awed as coffee, tea and oranges tumbled onto the bed along with the Coke cans, popcorn, the chocolate oranges and crisps, plus the still-dusty bottle of gin. Most extraordinary were the Roller-blades and the Game-Player with its tiny earphones and discs.

Swiftly she rigged up the player and, putting on the earphones, she sat down beside the boy and showed him how to play.

"It's brill!" he breathed and couldn't wait to try. When

he did, he became so absorbed Rosie had to pluck the earphones away from him.

"There's more to tell you," she said.

But he lifted one of the Rollerblades and turned their wheels in his hand. "Look at these! They're beauts! They're a bit like ice skates."

"They're not ice skates. You can use them on concrete."

"Are they yours, Rosie? Can I try them? What size are they?"

"They're size forty – a bit too big for me. My feet are thirty-eight."

"You're kidding!" Patrick looked at her feet. "Mine are six. I don't see how yours are thirty-eight. They don't look like planks."

"It's a different measurement. Let's compare."

They stretched their legs out until their feet were side by side. Patrick's were slightly bigger. Swiftly he took off one of his boots and tried a Rollerblade. "It fits!" he cried.

"Then you can have them," Rosie said.

His jaw dropped at the enormousness of her gift and for a moment he had trouble speaking. "Are you serious?" he said at last. "I mean, no one has anything like these! These are better than the best bicycle. Roller skates are nothing to these. My pals would give their bows and arrows and their catapults just for one go. They'd give their bogies for two goes! Are you sure you want to give them away? They must have been very expensive."

"About a hundred pounds," she said. "But I'll get Mum and Dad when they're in a good mood or they're watching the news and not listening properly to me and I'll tell them I left them somewhere."

"A hundred pounds!" Patrick choked. Swiftly he put on the other Rollerblade as though afraid she'd change her mind. He looked daft. "That's more than half a man's salary!"

"Oh. I didn't think a week's wages would be that good in 1943."

He stared at her. "They aren't. I was talking about a year's wages. And what do you mean, *watching* the news?"

She told him about television and his eyes rounded when he heard that quite often people his age had their own TVs in their bedrooms. "I don't though," she added, somewhat bitterly. "Mum thinks I'd do no homework if I had my own telly."

"And would you?"

She shrugged, then grinned. "I don't do much anyway. I told her it'd make no difference, but she won't give in. She's one sad person."

"Why? What happened to her?"

"Sorry?"

"Why is she sad? Did something bad happen?"

"No. Well, except for her not letting me have a TV. I just mean – no, never mind. It doesn't matter. What's a bogie, by the way?"

"A cart with ball-bearing wheels. You sit into it, on top of a hill, say, and someone gives you a push and you go whizzing down. Can I try one of these?"

He had picked up a packet of crisps and when she nodded, he opened one and tasted.

"Mmmm!" he said. "These are beautiful. We have ordinary potato crisps. There's no flavour, just a twist of salt to go with them. They're nice but these are delicious! It must be wonderful to live in your time, Rosie!"

As he munched away, she realised that he believed her story now. She took a deep breath and told him about Leonard Reddin and his efforts to get one thousand pounds from Edward. "I think he's a horrible man," she said. "I think he knows more about Mr Donovan's disappearance than he lets on. He said he'd call again and when he does I want to be here, in case he gives anything away."

"Why do you need my help?" Patrick rolled up the empty crisp bag and threw it in the wast bin.

"While he's busy calling here, you could go around to his house and search it."

He swallowed. "Break into his house, do you mean? And sneak around and look for evidence? And hope the neighbours don't hear me or he doesn't come back early and catch me? Is that what you want me to do?"

"Eh . . . yes." He made it sound dangerous.

Patrick clapped his hands. "Great! What an adventure! I've never done anything like this before, you know."

Taking the Rollerblades off he got up from the floor. He glanced at the clock on the bedside table and groaned. "It's nearly midnight. And we've all that digging to do tomorrow afternoon."

"What digging? I've never done any digging in my life!"

"Well, you will tomorrow. Digging and weeding and watering and planting all day long. I hate it."

"I was never any good at gardening," Rosie said firmly. "I'd make a mess of it. No point in my doing that kind of work."

Patrick laughed, "It's not gardening," he said. "You can't eat flowers and shrubs. It's a vegetable allotment. Even people who are no good at digging have to eat, don't they?

71

There's no other way to get turnips and cabbage and cauliflowers except by growing them."

Rosie groaned. She didn't even like those vegetables.

"Thanks for the Rollerblades," he said. "They really are the best present I've ever been given." He smiled from the doorway. "Do you know what?"

"What?"

"I take it back. You're not a bit like a girl."

She picked up an apple and with deadly accuracy fired it at his leg.

"That's not a compliment," she told him.

He looked at her dark eyes and ringlets, "You know what I mean. You're not afraid of much and you don't moan. You have Rollerblades. You do things!" He was becoming embarrassed, not used to paying compliments.

"That's what girls are like," Rosie said. "You just don't know any."

He looked at her, not teasing any more. "I'm getting to know you." Awkwardly he added, "You're good fun."

He closed the door quickly and Rosie smiled. Patrick was all right.

Chapter 9

Drowsily Rosie noted the clip-clop of horses' hooves and the clink of milk bottles on the doorstep. Darkness had faded but it wasn't yet day. She felt she'd been asleep for only a few minutes. When she looked at the clock she saw it was only six am. Gratefully she drifted off again.

A little while later she woke with a start. Someone was singing – or trying to sing – about laundry. As far as she could make out, he wanted to hang out his clothes on the Siegfried line, whatever that was. She must be dreaming. Who'd be bothered writing a song about washing? And "song" hardly described the awful sound. Now the voice was coming up the garden path, screeching for dirty laundry.

Have you any dirty washing, Mother dee-ar?

The man must be in horrible pain, she thought.

The bell rang. "Any waste paper, Missus?"

Maria murmured something and it was a minute or two before Rosie heard, "Thanks very much, Missus. God bless you."

The door closed and the awful singing began again as the man left. Looking out the window she could see a horse drawing a cart stacked with paper. Rosie got back into bed.

Someone should tell that fellow to get voice lessons. Someone should tell him he ought to give up singing. His voice was horrible, and she should know, being a singer of unmatched awfulness. Not that she'd ever wanted to sing and indeed the choir teacher in her old primary school had always encouraged this reluctance. But people often used to ask her for a song, especially in the past where they went in for home entertainment. They didn't take no for an answer. Then they couldn't hide the shock at her failure to get a note right. She sincerely hoped nobody would insist that she sing this time.

It was daylight now and the neighbourhood was already busy. Rosie could hear people walking smartly down the street. Where were they all going on a Saturday morning? It was only nine o'clock. She snoozed off once more.

> *Scrap metal, any scrap metal?*
> *Give us an iron, give us a kettle,*
> *Find an oul pot, find an oul pan*
> *And hand them over to the scrap-metal man,*
> *Any oul lawnmowers left in the rain?*
> *Give them all to the Hammond Lane,*
> *We want iron, we want tin,*
> *We even want your metal bin.*
> *Scrap metal, any scrap metal?*
> *Scrap metal, any scrap metal?*

This time the voice was a chant and the man did not call to the houses. Instead he walked up the road, leading his horse and cart, intoning the same sing-song over and over. Every so often he'd stop as a housewife hailed him and then Rosie could hear the sound of metal clanging in the cart. His voice was also metallic as if the tin and iron had entered his system. It grated on Rosie's nerves and although it was fading in the distance she was thoroughly awake now.

What was she going to do about clothes? From her experience she knew people in the past didn't change their clothes that often. The fact that they didn't have washing-machines and dryers probably had a lot to do with it. But it would be nice to wear something different at least once before she went home.

Then, like an answer to her hopes, Maria knocked on the door and entered, carrying some dresses and underwear.

"Rosie, I don't want you to be embarrassed, but Edward told me you had no time to pack yesterday. Something about your father having to rush off and your having to leave in a hurry . . . To be honest, I couldn't make much sense of it all. But Edward was never one to speak clearly first thing in the day. Indeed he prefers not to speak at all till mid-morning. Says his thoughts are still muddled with sleep. I myself am the opposite. Just listen to me gabbling away! Anyway, Mrs Kennedy has given me a couple of things her daughter, Frances, wore when she was younger. She's gone away now to America – Frances, that is – not Mrs Kennedy!"

At long last Maria paused and put the clothes on top of the chest of drawers and turned again to Rosie. About to say something else, her jaw dropped. Then she closed and opened her mouth a number of times, unable to speak. Swallowing, she pointed and Rosie looked. Last night she'd been too tired to bother putting away the contents of her rucksack and had just stacked them on the floor, except for the Game-Player which she'd pushed into a drawer.

"Wh-what – ? How – ? Is that – ?" Maria was unable to frame the question, swallowing her words in astonishment.

"Oh, I brought those with the bananas. They're for you and Edward and Patrick."

"For us?" Swiftly Maria moved to the other side of the bed. "For us? But where did you get all this? No, don't answer! I must mind my own business. I suppose I *should* care if your father is dealing on the black market, but I don't. I don't! Things have just been too difficult. My God! This is marvellous. Tea! Proper tea! Do you know how precious this is, you wonderful child?"

She held up the carton and kissed it. Then she opened it and Rosie saw her puzzlement. "They're tea bags," Rosie explained. "One tea bag will make a pot of tea for two people."

"That's a very clever idea for the Emergency," said Maria. "What a good way to make sure no tea leaves are wasted! Especially now there's such a shortage and we're allowed only half an ounce per person per week."

Maria set down the tea and studied the other items. "Oh look! You brought coffee! It's so hard to get. And sugar! And fruit! Oranges are really scarce. And crisps and cans of drink. What's Coca-Cola? And what on earth are these? Chocolate oranges – my, my! This is all too much to take in. Just look at this fruit! And what's this bag of grain?" She studied the Cellophane pack. *Makes more than a bucket of popcorn*. "Good Heavens. I've heard of popcorn! It's American isn't it? I didn't know you could get it in Ireland!"

Before Rosie could comment, Maria noticed something else. "I can't believe it," She shrieked. "Gin! No one can get gin! The distilleries in Britain are making hardly any. Look at that huge bottle! Oh, Rosie, this is just smashing!"

She sat down suddenly on the girl's bed.

"It's nothing," Rosie muttered, feeling embarrassed. All she'd had to do was open the cupboards at home and everything was there. She could have brought twice as much and felt sorry now that she hadn't.

"This is *not* nothing, Rosie." Maria was still overwhelmed. "This is – this is extraordinary! I don't know how to thank you."

She sat for a moment, lovingly holding the tea and the gin and the coffee and staring at the rest. Her face was thoughtful. "Does Edward know you've brought all this?" she asked slowly.

Rosie shook her head.

"Well, don't tell him. He might disapprove. Oh, I know he said your father's activities on the black market were his own business, but he was just being polite."

"We can't leave him out," Rosie objected, visualising Maria, Patrick and herself guzzling secretively in her room while Edward wondered where they all were.

"Of course we can't. But I won't have him getting on his high horse and insisting all of these lovely things go back to where they came from."

Rosie stayed silent, unable to say these weren't black-market goods, yet thinking it was all a bit hard on Edward.

"What I want to do – if you have no objection, Rosie – is to have a surprise party for Edward's birthday next Thursday. We'll ask some friends and neighbours. Edward won't be able to raise questions till afterwards and by then it will be too late to do anything. What do you think?"

"I think that's a great idea."

"Good. Edward's gone to the office, so I'll bring everything downstairs and hide it. We can have the fruit today since it won't keep."

"And maybe we could try some popcorn," Rosie said. Popcorn was one of her favourite foods at the moment. "There's loads of it. And maybe we could share a chocolate orange? Or eat some crisps?" She couldn't bear the thought of more mashed parsnips.

Immediately Maria was apologetic. "I'm very sorry, Rosie. I'm forgetting all these belong to you and here I am forcing you to do what I want. Of course you must take whatever you wish."

At once Rosie felt ashamed. In less than a week she'd be home and able to have whatever sweets or food she wanted. "I think we should keep everything for the party except some of the popcorn."

Maria smiled and said as she went out the door, "I feel as if Santa Claus has visited us right in the middle of July!"

Porridge was really quite nice, Rosie thought, especially with the cream from the top of the bottle and some sugar. And the milk was delicious, much richer than any she'd ever tasted. Maria told her to have as much as she wanted and as much butter as she liked on the dark bread. There was no shortage of dairy products.

"Would you like to play handball?" Patrick asked when she'd finished.

"I thought we were going to the allotment?"

"Not till after dinner. Da's at work this morning." He saw the question in her eyes. "Everyone works on Saturday mornings," he told her. "Offices close at half twelve, but the shops open again in the afternoon."

"You'll have to show me how to play handball."

"And you'll have to help me with the Rollerblades, Rosie."

A few minutes later on the front doorstep, Patrick handed Rosie his boots and put on the Rollerblades. As they made their way along Griffith Avenue, he leaned heavily against her. Every so often he let go and tried to find his balance.

"It's easier if you go faster," Rosie told him as once again his feet travelled in opposite directions. Holding his boots made it difficult for her to keep him upright. But when he tried to do as she directed, the blades crossed each other and tripped him up.

"You're looking down," she said. "If you look down you'll lose your balance."

At last he seemed to get the hang of it and began to skate with confidence. Turning his head he shouted, "I can do it. Look at *me*!"

"Oh no! Watch out!" Rosie saw Mrs Kennedy. She was carrying a shopping bag and stopped dead. Patrick saw her too, but far too late. Having no idea how to brake, he tried to go round her. At the same time she went to step out of his way and ended up right in his path. In an effort to save himself and at the same time not send Mrs Kennedy flying, he threw his arms around her and struggled to keep both of them upright. To Rosie they looked like two drunks staggering across the path. Colliding with a large elm tree they fell in a heap. By the time Rosie reached them, they were attempting to untangle themselves.

Mrs Kennedy's shopping had fallen out of the bag and one of her shoes had come off. Red-faced, she sat under the tree, puffing and panting. As soon as her breath returned she whacked the boy with a loaf of bread and roared, "If you want to hug someone in the street, young Patrick, you don't have to try and run them over first. Charging at me like a steam-train and then dragging me all over the place – *oh ha ha* – what are you doing, young one? Stop. You're tickling my foot, Rosie! *Ha ha oh ha* – stop it!" She lashed out at the girl who was attempting to put on her shoe. Then, scrambling to her feet, she saw their dismayed faces and began to calm down. She smiled. "I should be thanking my lucky stars, I suppose. I've never before had a young fella make a mad dash to throw his arms around me. Not even Mr Kennedy in his heyday! You should've seen the look of panic on your face, young Patrick!" She began to giggle. Rosie remembered Patrick's confident expression as he shouted back and she too started laughing.

Mrs Kennedy was guffawing now and had to clutch the tree with the pain. Rosie was gulping and clutching Mrs Kennedy. Patrick didn't see the funny side. He tried to stand up but his legs went flying and the other two collapsed in hysterics. The only way he could get to his feet was by putting his arms around the tree and easing himself up.

"Well, aren't you mad about hugging today, young Patrick," Mrs Kennedy managed. "If it's not me, it's the tree. Poor Rosie here, no doubt now she feels left out!"

At his look of intense outrage Rosie and Mrs Kennedy started again and it was some minutes before they calmed down.

"Oh dear Lord!" Mrs Kennedy wiped the tears away. "That was a good laugh. Oh dear, oh dear!" As she walked away they could hear bouts of laughter until she reached her own door.

But from here on, once he'd been told how to brake, Patrick managed the Rollerblades so well Rosie had to run after him. He was an object of great attention, with people nudging each other and turning to stare at his footwear. One man stood in his path and Patrick glided to a stop, as if he'd had a lifetime of rollerblading.

"Where did you get those?" the man asked, his curiosity urgent.

"My pal here gave them to me. They're a present."

The man turned to Rosie. "They're smashing! I've never seen anything like them. Did you get them in Dublin?"

Rosie shook her head. "Not really. You can't buy them here."

The man's voice became a whisper, "Did you get them on the black market? I'd pay a lot for a pair. Listen, here's a quid. Just tell me your source. A contact is all I need!"

Rosie stared at him, bewildered. His hand went to his pocket again. "A fiver then? A name is all I want. Surely that's worth a fiver. And you needn't worry. I'll keep my mouth shut."

"I don't know what you're talking about," Rosie said.

Patrick tugged on her arm and skated off. She ran after him and the man shouted, "A tenner, then. I'll give you a tenner. Come back here! We'll come to an arrangement . . ."

But they were gone, taking his hopes of vast profits with them. He sighed. "People could've used them to get into work. Postmen would've done their rounds quicker.

Housewives could've gone for their shopping much faster. A name was all I wanted. It wasn't much to ask, was it?" Dreams shattered, he stared into space.

Very soon Patrick and Rosie were down the hill, into St. Patrick's College and at the handball alley.

Patrick was putting on his runners when a huge wailing noise began. The sound waves vibrated in the air all around them. Rosie held her hands over her ears. "What on earth is that?" she asked. "It sounds like a million ambulances!"

"Oh, it's just the air-raid siren in the city," Patrick told her.

Rosie remembered from her history book vague details of a bomb dropped on Dublin during the war. It wasn't about to fall on them, was it? Was this the warning signal?

Her imagination worked overtime. They were sitting ducks in the handball alley, she thought. Any low-flying pilot could see them. In a panic she looked around for shelter and would have rushed from the alley had Patrick not grabbed her arm.

"It's all right," he said. "There won't be any bomb. One fell two years ago in the North Strand, but the Germans said that was an accident."

"Well, if there's no danger why have an air-raid siren that could kill you with the shock?" Rosie was both puzzled and annoyed.

"In case there's another accident, which probably won't happen. It's to get people used to using the bomb shelters."

Reassured by his calm, Rosie walked out of the handball alley. Within a couple of minutes she returned. "What bomb shelters? I don't see anything that looks like a bomb shelter."

"That's 'cos they only have them in town where there are crowds, though my pal, Macker, has one in his back garden. His da built it. He sometimes lets us use it for a den, when his ma's not around."

Rosie was fascinated. "Their own personal bomb shelter! I'd love to see it."

"I'll ask him. He and Johnno should be here any minute. I'd better show you how to play before they come."

He took a smooth rubber ball from his pocket. It was slightly bigger than a squash ball. He drove it against the front wall and each time it returned, whacked it with the palm of his hand. Rosie noticed that the ball got more bouncy with every impact and soon it was flying to and from the boy's hand. Patrick stopped. "Now it's warmed up," he said. "I have the first hand-in. That means I have first serve. I hit the ball to the wall and it can only hit the ground once before you return it. If you miss or let it bounce more than once, then I get a point and it's still my hand-in. But if I miss your return or the ball hops more than once then it's your hand-in and you can score points. We'll play to nine. The first person to reach nine wins, right?"

"Okay," Rosie said, not sure she understood, but dying to have a go.

She missed every one of Patrick's serves. "The ball is too small," she moaned. She was running all over the court and could not get a shot in. "My hand is too small," she panted. "I need a bat."

Behind her a voice jeered, "You couldn't hit it with a tennis racquet!" Rosie turned to see two boys grinning at her.

"If you want to have a real game, you can play me," the

taller one addressed Patrick. "And the winner plays Johnno." He looked scornfully at Rosie, "I suppose the loser could play your mot here!"

Patrick went beetroot and said, "Rosie's not my mot. She's my pal. And if anyone else says she's my girlfriend, I'll – I'll spifflicate them so I will!"

Rosie wasn't sure whether she should feel flattered or offended. It was nice of Patrick to say she was his friend. But wasn't it a bit of an insult, threatening to bash up anyone who said she was his girlfriend?

"I don't want to be your – your mot," she said rather feebly. What kind of a word was 'mot' anyway? It sounded like an insect.

The two boys grinned away, but added no further fuel to the flames.

Watching Patrick and Macker play, Rosie could see how skilful they were. They tried to outwit each other with drop shots, overheads and slammers, rarely failing to connect with the ball. In the end Macker won by a point, then went on to beat Johnno, a much quieter boy who had little conversation, but just grinned all the time.

When Patrick played Rosie, the other two stood at the back, Macker passing smart remarks:

"You should be tap-dancing in those shoes!"

"Oh what a lovely shot! Pity you hit the wrong wall."

"Your curls move faster than you. They're bouncing more than the ball!"

The reference to her hair was the last straw. She ignored Patrick's next shot and was striding towards Macker when the ball bounced off the wall and whacked her on the back of the head.

"Oh, well done!" Macker jeered. "That's what I call using your head. Well hit! You should keep your back turned all the time – you play better that way!" He roared laughing, while Johnno grinned away.

Rosie marched past him. He was very mean, she thought. It was her first time to play and she wasn't hanging around to put up with these insults. She went to where Patrick had left the Rollerblades on the other side of the alley, and put them on quickly.

Clumsily she made her way down the short gravel path to where the boys were standing, Macker still making comments: "Janey, you can't move, can you, never mind play handball?"

I'll show him! Rosie thought and once she reached the smooth concrete she took off. On flying wheels, she raced around the alley, until she had gathered speed. Then, hoping she wasn't going to make a complete fool of herself, she took the wall at an angle, managing to climb about five feet before curving back down. Jump-landing, she closed her eyes in gratitude as she came down on her feet, then made for the boys.

Macker was open-mouthed and Johnno had stopped grinning as she turned in ever decreasing circles around them. Macker was beginning to look a bit scared of the whirlwind closing in on him. But Rosie barely brushed his arm before racing down the smooth drive, taking the three steps with apparent ease.

"That's brill, Rosie!" She heard Patrick shout and did a quick turn to wave before taking off once more and making for home.

She wasn't waiting around for that horrible Macker. Remembering his last gobsmacked expression, Rosie smiled.

Chapter 10

Dinner was at one o'clock and Rosie thought it looked awful. Her hopes had been raised when Patrick told her they were having coddle and explained that this was sausages, rashers, onions and potatoes. Rosie quite liked all of these and reckoned it would be impossible to spoil them. Her disappointment was huge when a large soup bowl of sticky white liquid was put in front of her. She could make out the shape of different lumps beneath the surface.

"I thought you said we were having sausages and rashers," she whispered.

"We are," Patrick was already eating with gusto.

"Well, where are they?" Rosie thought the mixture in front of her resembled lumpy wallpaper paste.

"In front of you. In the bowl."

Rosie prodded the mixture. The sausages were white and the rashers not much better. And the mix looked horrible.

"Coddle is one of Patrick's favourite dinners," Maria told her. "I had no white flour to thicken the sauce when I'd boiled the ingredients, so I had to use cornflour. It might be a little thick, but I hope you like it."

Boiled the ingredients! How could someone do that to sausages and rashers? This food had been specially invented for frying, not for boiling white and sticking in white glue.

Still . . . it smelled nice. And the other three were eating with great enthusiasm.

Carefully, Rosie tasted a mouthful. Not bad. She tried again, closing her eyes to the unnaturally pale ingredients. It was delicious if you didn't look at it. She found herself eating every morsel and, like the others, using bread to mop up the last of the sauce.

"That was really nice." She sighed with satisfaction. "I think it was the most beautiful dinner I've ever tasted."

Edward smiled at her, "There's nothing like a good coddle to give you the strength for hard labour."

Rosie groaned.

Edward had borrowed Mrs Kennedy's bike for her. The neighbour said she could have it until she went home. It was strong and black and very heavy. Rosie cycled up the steep hill towards Santry, noticing that the school and hotel weren't yet built. The green meadows on either side made her feel she was journeying through the countryside. And that impression was increased when they came to the allotment. It was where Whitehall church would later be. Now, in its place was a huge field, with row upon row of vegetables and a number of sheds along the margin. Families were already working on the different allotments.

Edward collected some implements from one of the sheds. "Now, Rosie," he said, "you're the guest, so you have a choice of jobs. You can weed, or pick potatoes, onions and turnips, or dig in some manure for the late cabbages."

None of them sounded attractive. She thought of

suggesting that a guest should have the privilege of doing nothing, but it didn't seem to be an option. "I'll dig in the manure," she said.

Edward hauled over some sacks from the edge of the field. "Empty them out along those four rows," he pointed. "Then spread the manure and dig it in."

Rosie approached one of the sacks and nearly gagged. "There's a terrible smell," she said.

"What do you expect?" Patrick laughed. "It's good strong horse manure, not perfume. It's supposed to pong!"

"Well, it's shocking," Rosie muttered. But she set about up-ending the sack, trying to hold her nose at the same time.

"You're putting it all over your shoes!" Patrick told her.

"Oh God albighty! Id's rebolting. Look ad id. Id's all wed."

"It's not wet; it's just a bit damp. You'll have to stop holding your nose and use your two hands if you don't want to get the stuff all over you."

Rosie took his advice. "It's more than damp!" She watched a splodge of manure ooze over her foot, then set to work, sighing.

Already Maria and Edward were busy examining their crop, deciding what to pick, and Patrick was on his knees, weeding. "You chose the best job, Rosie," he stated. "You might smell like a farmyard afterwards, but you won't be in awful pain, like me. Your muscles will work, not like mine. You'll be able to stand up straight without creaking, not like me. Your fingernails will be clean, not like mine. You'll be able to grip your knife and hold your spoon at teatime, not like me. People will run a mile from your horrible pong but at least you'll –"

"Oh, *shut up!*" Rosie told him. The boy grinned.

They worked away for a couple of hours. The mix of heat and smell had Rosie trying not to breathe. The back of her neck and legs were burning in the afternoon sun. She was beginning to feel a little sick when Edward called over, "Time for a cuppa, Rosie. You're doing a great job there."

Looking up, she saw Edward making for the shed. Maria had placed a blanket on the grass outside. Gratefully the girl sat down. All around, other families were taking their break.

Maria handed her a rasher sandwich and a bottle of cold tea. Rosie drank thirstily and gulped the food. Afterwards she thought she'd never ever had a break where the food had been so delicious. Who'd have thought that cold tea could taste better than Coke or orange? She must try it when she got home.

'Dad would be so amazed if he saw me now,' Rosie thought as she finished spreading the manure and put away the sacks and shovel in the shed. She remembered her father's efforts at getting her to take an interest in gardening. She'd used every excuse to get out of mowing: like the grass was so green it gave her a headache; or the lawnmower didn't cut properly and had a very patchy effect; or it had gone mad altogether and dug up large clumps of soil.

Mr McGrath would often sigh when he saw the results of his daughter's latest efforts and he would not ask her to garden for a long while afterwards. Certainly he'd never believe she could spread manure properly and without complaint.

Not that she didn't want to complain. But she was too exhausted. Patrick had been wrong about how she'd feel.

Every part of her ached. She'd never be able to use her arms or shoulders again without incredible pain.

On their way home, her legs were so tired she could barely get the bicycle pedals to go round. Luckily the journey was downhill. Once inside the house on Griffith Avenue, she saw the others wrinkle their faces at the smell she'd brought home and, although exhausted, she hastily excused herself, limped upstairs and locked herself in the bathroom.

Since there was no hot water, Rosie decided there was nothing for it but to have a cold bath. It was an experience she never wanted to repeat, especially as the soap was a thick hard slab that smelled of disinfectant and raised hardly any lather. When she was finished she noticed all the clay and manure were transferred onto the surface of the bath and she spent another quarter of an hour cleaning.

By the time she came downstairs she was almost weeping with exhaustion. But a plateful of hot crispy chips and a cup of proper tea restored some of her energy. And when Edward said, "You were a great help today, Rosie," she stretched back with satisfaction until Patrick added by way of comfort, "At least you won't be all smelly when you come home after turf-cutting tomorrow!"

Oh God, she groaned. At this rate she'd be returning to the future on a stretcher.

As she and Patrick washed up the dishes in the kitchen, the boy told her, "Macker says you can visit his bomb shelter, if you want."

"Macker's a pain in the neck," Rosie said, fed up with life again. "That was my first time to play handball and all he could do was sneer."

"Macker's all right," Patrick defended his friend. "He didn't know you'd never played before. Anyway, he thinks you're brill now. He couldn't believe it when he saw you on the Rollerblades. He was dead sorry for jeering you."

"Why? Does he want a go on them?"

"Yes, he does. I never let on they were mine and told him he'd have to ask you. So he said you could visit his bomb shelter any time and he says he'll give you his five best gullies if he can try the Rollerblades."

"Sorry? His five best what?"

"Gullies. Big marbles. They're great for striking the small ones. Massive ball-bearings they are!"

"I don't play marbles. He can keep his gullies and his ball-bearings, so he can!"

At once Patrick's tone was pleading. "Rosie, please! You can take them and give them to me! He has the best marbles around. His uncle got them from the ball-bearing factory where he works. No one else has the like of them."

Rosie found it difficult to get worked up about marbles but to please Patrick she agreed to do a deal with Macker.

At that moment she noticed all the gas jets on the cooker were still lit. Since there was nothing on any of them she went to turn off the gas.

"Don't do that!" Patrick stopped her. "We have to leave it on the glimmer."

"Why?"

"If you turn it off, you use too much gas switching it back on. It's to save gas."

Rosie had one of her bright ideas. "Why don't we make some popcorn? It'll only take a few minutes and it's delicious!"

91

Patrick was tempted. "I've never tasted popcorn," he said. "But we're not supposed to cook after eight o'clock at night."

"We have five minutes, so. It won't take much longer than that."

Patrick needed no further prompting, but they couldn't find the popcorn in any of the cupboards.

"Your mum is hiding all the stuff I gave her," Rosie muttered as they searched.

"Oh! It'll be in the piano in the sitting-room then. Or under the sofa." Patrick disappeared and was back in a few seconds with the popcorn.

Rosie put some butter in the bottom of a pot, raised the gas, and as the butter melted, Patrick poured in the grains.

"Stop! That's more than enough." Swiftly Rosie put the lid on. In a few minutes the contents began to pop and Patrick's curiosity got the better of him. He lifted the lid and the white fluffy popcorn shot out at him.

"What are you doing?" Rosie cried.

He could not get the lid back on.

"Get a bigger pot!" she yelled.

In the dining-room, listening to the radio, Patrick's parents heard shouting and the clanging of pots. Both adults rushed into the kitchen. The doorbell rang but no one heard. Nor did they hear Mrs Kennedy yelling through the letterbox, "The glimmer man is coming! The glimmer man is coming!"

Patrick had at last got a bigger pot and Rosie emptied the still-popping corn into it and fastened the lid tightly.

"We saved nearly all of it," she said brightly. "There's only a bit on the floor."

"What on earth are you doing?" Maria asked.

There was no time to answer. Somebody banged on the back door before swinging it open. An official-looking man with a notebook stepped in. Right behind him was the flustered figure of Mrs Kennedy.

"Glimmer man!" said the official tersely. He waved an identification card.

"I tried to warn you," said Mrs Kennedy. "I rang the doorbell, rapped on the knocker and roared through the letterbox. And I tried to engage this wee gentleman in polite conversation, but sure he went galloping around the side passage without a by-your-leave!"

"As what I am entitled to!" The glimmer man was irate. He turned to Maria. "It's obvious to me, Missus, that youse are in breach of the gas regulations and that youse are cooking, which means the gas supplies to this house can be cut off on youse forthwith!"

"Only a louser would cut off people's gas supplies!" Mrs Kennedy was indignant. "What kind of bowsy are you, to be doing that for a living?"

"A very mean bowsy," Rosie observed. "It's only a few minutes past eight and we'd have been finished if Patrick hadn't put too much popcorn in the pot."

"Youse are not getting away with calling me a louser and a bowsy – what did youse say youse were cooking?"

"Popcorn," said Rosie.

"It's beautiful," Patrick added.

"There's enough for all of us," his mum said.

"Why don't youse – you – join us?" Edward smiled.

"Only a bowsy would refuse," murmured Mrs Kennedy, adding quickly, "And you don't look like a bowsy, Mister.

You look like a soft-hearted wee man who wouldn't punish a family just because the wee children made a mistake. Amn't I right now? Don't I know the type of you?" She scooped a few of the spilt popcorn from the counter and put them in her mouth. Then she closed her eyes. "Mister, I'm telling you, you've a treat in store!"

It was obvious the glimmer man was weakening. He sniffed the air appreciatively and said, "Well, I wouldn't want to be rude to youse and turn down any invite youse are making, specially to partake of popcorn, what I have never had the pleasure of tasting. So, in order that youse won't think I am either a louser or a bowsy, I will sit down with youse, so I will."

At once Maria ushered him into the dining-room. Patrick got out six bowls, Edward carried in the pot and Rosie found a big ladle.

Soon they were all tucking into the warm popcorn.
"'S beautiful!" said Mrs Kennedy and they all sighed with satisfaction. There was enough for second helpings and soon the glimmer man was telling them about the tragedy that was his life. Nobody liked him, he said. Nobody wanted him calling to their door. He was never welcome. The minute he was seen in the neighbourhood everyone went running to warn everyone else. People rushed to turn down the gas when he called and used wet tea towels to cool the gas rings. People were afraid of him. Even his friends treated him with suspicion. It was very depressing. So it was wonderful to meet such kind people as themselves, salt-of-the-earth types who invited him in and were nice to him. Really, he was overcome at all this niceness –

Here the glimmer man took a fit of emotional gulping

and Mrs Kennedy patted him on the back, murmuring, "There, there! Sure we never meant to call you a bowsy. Or indeed a louser. And you're not one bit mean. You're a decent wee man, so y'are, and don't be mindin' anyone who says different."

At last the man left, blowing his nose and vowing never to forget their kindness. All of them waved him down the garden path, with Mrs Kennedy muttering, "Dear me, dear me. What sort of softies are the Gas Board employing? That poor wee man was nearly crying."

All of a sudden Rosie was overcome by tiredness and thought she would fall over if she didn't lie down. She said goodnight as the two women chatted on the doorstep.

"You'd best go to bed too, Patrick," Maria said. "You both have a hard day tomorrow."

Deciding not to draw the curtains, Rosie lay in bed watching the night sky, a twinkling tapestry of stars, with the almost-full moon gazing at her, calm and still. Not a cloud cast a shadow, not a breeze murmured. It occurred to Rosie that the world and its setting were wonderful. And before she fell asleep she thought how perfect everything would be if people like Leonard Reddin either didn't exist or were completely different.

Chapter 11

When Edward called them for eight o'clock Mass in Corpus Christi Church, Rosie thought he was joking. In 2001 she went to Sunday Mass at midday. And sometimes her parents forgot about church, especially if they'd been out late the night before.

"Do we have to go?" she asked Edward. "I'm very tired."

"Don't be silly, Rosie. You must make the effort. After all, it's only once a week."

Rosie protested, "But why do I have to make the effort so early? It must be cockcrow."

"It's half seven. And we're up early because we're spending the day on the bog, remember?"

"Oh God!" she moaned. "And what about breakfast? Are we not having any?"

"Plenty of time for breakfast after Mass."

"You've no hat, Rosie!" Maria stopped her on the way out.

"I don't wear hats, not in July," the girl told her.

"But you have to wear one to Mass! I'll get you one of mine."

And off she went, returning with what looked like a pink cowboy hat sporting three long feathers in the front.

This is *so* bad! Rosie thought. This is going to be such a rotten day. Getting up at dawn and having to wear this rotten, rotten hat!

With very bad grace, she snatched it from Maria and plonked it on.

"That really suits you," Patrick was smirking. "You look like Annie-Get-Your-Gun, the greatest cowgirl in the West!" he sniggered.

They were bound to be the only ones at Mass, she thought, and was surprised to see that the huge church was crowded. The men were dressed in suits and the women in their Sunday best. And every female wore a scarf or hat while every man was bareheaded, hat in hand.

As they arrived the congregation stood up, the organ played and everyone sang with great gusto:

Sweet Heart of Jesus
Font of love and mercy
To thee we cry
Our blessings to restore!

Rosie groaned. She knew this hymn because Dad, whenever he told her about his childhood, would end up singing it. It was the only hymn he knew and Rosie thought it had the dreariest most miserable melody of any tune she had ever heard.

From the first line Maria was at her to join in. "We have to show reverence. Sing up, Rosie! I'm sure you have a lovely voice!"

On the other side of his wife, Edward's eyes widened and

97

lifted to heaven. He had heard Rosie sing once before, in 1920. He would never forget the sound. It wasn't an experience anyone present would appreciate and he prayed that she would stay silent.

Rosie was very willing to keep her voice to herself, but Maria gave her a rather painful dig which made her grit her teeth and think, "Okay, you asked for it!"

Taking a deep breath she sang with determination – and with a terrible shrillness:

> *Oh touch our hearts*
> *So cold and so ungrateful*
> *And make us Lo-or- or- rd –*
> *Thine o-wen forever mo-wer!*

It was the end of the verse and she stopped. Around her there was a stunned hush and people were gaping at her. Rosie did the only thing she could think of. She had a fit of coughing. Edward mouthed a 'thank you' towards the ceiling. Patrick tried to control his laughter and Maria stayed in shock for some minutes.

As soon as the congregation sat down, Mass began. Rosie found the priest's voice so soothing she dozed off. Every so often Maria gave her a nudge to stand up, kneel down or sit on the seat. This made her so grumpy that at one point she hissed, "What's the point in staying awake? I don't understand one word the priest's saying."

And Maria hissed back, "Just because it's Latin doesn't mean you don't have to take part!"

Rosie, still sleepy, said without thinking. "Latin? No wonder I can't follow. Dad said Latin isn't allowed any more. Why isn't it in English?"

Maria wondered whether the girl had taken leave of her senses. Whoever heard of a Mass in English? It wouldn't be right or proper. Had Rosie any religion at all? Before she could say a word, Edward whispered, "She's a bit dopey because she was asleep. She knows you don't have Mass in English."

The words were loud enough for Rosie to hear and she copped on immediately. "Of course it's Latin!" she whispered. " I'm so stupid. Sorry, Maria, I wasn't properly awake and I got mixed up."

Maria frowned, but by now people were turning around again and a few of them said 'Hush!' so she did not question the girl.

Rosie stayed awake, managing to concentrate so well that she knew when to turn, and shake Maria's hand, murmuring, "Peace be with you."

The poor woman was so startled she replied, "And how are you keeping yourself?" Then she bit her lip and gave Rosie some very funny looks.

"She thinks there's something up," Rosie realised, noticing too late that no one else was shaking hands.

At the end of the Mass people rose for the final hymn, which was the same one as before. Rosie saw this as an opportunity to set any doubts Maria had about her religion at rest. So she sang with great enthusiasm, getting a bit carried away towards the end:

> *Sweet Heart of Jesus*
> *We implore*
> *Oh make us love thee-ee-ee*
> *More and mo-ow-ow-ow-ow-ere*

This time people put their hands over their ears, waiting

for the torture to stop. One woman looked pleadingly at Rosie, tears in her eyes. Patrick too wept, but from uncontrollable mirth. Edward didn't know whether to laugh or cry and his wife wished she could disappear – or better still that Rosie could disappear.

The girl missed every reaction, her eyes closed in fervour. When she opened them she was mildly surprised to see most of the people around her were hurrying out of their seats and down the aisle.

The woman with tears in her eyes murmured forgivingly to her husband, "She didn't sound right, did she? Maybe the poor child was in agony."

"Not in as much agony as me!" Her husband was not at all forgiving. "I'll always remember that screeching. It'll give me nightmares for years."

In the room behind the altar the priest asked, "Who on earth was that child with the extraordinary voice?"

"I don't know, Father," said the altar boy, who had been rather impressed by Rosie's performance, "but her singing was powerful."

The priest caught his admiring tone and looked at him pityingly, "Oh, it was powerful all right. Mark my words, that girl could get a job in Hollywood, in the pictures. She could star with Bella Lugosi as Dracula's crow."

"Did you think she was that good, Father?" The altar boy was astonished and wished that he could meet the girl Father Daly said could one day be a film star.

By the time they'd left the church Maria had decided to say nothing to Rosie about the last half hour. She wanted to forget it and hoped no one would ever bring up the subject again.

After a breakfast of porridge, rashers and sausages and fried bread, Rosie sat back and said to Patrick, "Now I'm able to face anything."

"Not like all the people who heard your singing!" the boy grinned.

"Patrick! We will not discuss Rosie's singing!" Maria was grim. "You are not to ruin a beautiful day."

Rosie changed into shorts and an old blouse and swopped her patent shoes for a pair of runners belonging to Patrick. It was a relief to feel so comfortable. Maria made a packed lunch and saw them to the door.

"Aren't you coming with us?" Rosie asked.

"No. Mrs Doyle isn't feeling so well and I promised I'd make her some dinner and keep her company. It's such a beautiful day though, I wish I were going with you."

If Rosie had known Mrs Doyle she'd have offered to change places with Maria. Instead she got up on the bicycle, her muscles screeching, and moaned to herself when Edward said, "We should be over at the Featherbed beyond Rathfarnham in an hour or so."

It was a glorious day and Rosie's spirits lifted as they freewheeled down Drumcondra, gathering enough speed to take the small hills in their stride. O'Connell Street was almost empty, the shops closed. She saw the squat concrete shelters Patrick had mentioned but was much more fascinated by Nelson's Pillar, stopping near the base to gaze up at the imposing statue. Nelson's lordly hand, held high above the city, seemed to state, "I am master of all I survey."

Edward stopped beside her. "You'd think you'd never seen Nelson before," he said.

"This was blown up in 1963," she told him.

Astonished, Edward too gazed upwards. "What happened?" His heart sank. "Don't tell me there's going to be another war?"

"No, nothing like that. I think it was the IRA. who blew it up. Dad said no one was killed and he said there was no violence or trouble afterwards."

Edward looked at the magnificent column with some sadness. "I used to make appointments with Maria to meet here when we were keeping company," he said. "Lots of young couples still do the same. It's one of the most favoured meeting places in Ireland. Everyone knows Nelson's Pillar. Such a pity to think of it being destroyed. Will it be rebuilt?"

"No, but they'll put another statue in its place."

"What kind of statue? A patriot? A famous person? An angel like on the O'Connell monument? Or perhaps a saint?"

"Eh, no, not any of them. Er, I don't remember the real name for what they put up. It's called the Floosy in the Jacuzzi."

"Sorry? The what?" Edward's shock was obvious. "Are you telling me they're going to put up a statue of a floosy – of a shameless woman – in place of Nelson? I can't believe it! And what's a jacuzzi?"

"It's eh – it's a bath."

Edward's expression was one of disbelief. He stared hard at Rosie, but it was clear she wasn't joking. "A woman in a bath? Instead of Nelson? Respectable people won't want to meet beside a floosy in a bathtub! I can't believe this. It's insane!"

Before Rosie could tell him not to worry, the floosy

would in her turn be replaced by a giant needle, Edward was up on his saddle and cycling off in a huff. He passed the waiting Patrick without a word. When Rosie caught up on the boy, he asked, "What did you say to Da? He went by me and all I could hear was *'Disgraceful! Mad! A floosy!'* He wasn't talking about you, was he?"

Rosie shook her head but felt unable to explain. She was saved the trouble when Edward shouted back at them to get a move on, that the day would be gone before any work was done.

"I don't know what you said, but Da's in very bad form," Patrick said.

However, Rosie was cycling furiously ahead and didn't seem to hear.

By the time they got to Rathfarnham, Edward had recovered his temper and he slowed down to point out the hill they must climb, towards Glencree and the Featherbed. Rosie reckoned she'd never make it. Hell must be a matter of climbing steep hills forever, she thought.

But at last Patrick stopped and got off his bike near an old thatched cottage. Beyond it stretched the bogland, broken here and there with whin bushes and heather. In the distance, high on the hillside, was a small forest of pine trees.

Rosie peered upland, one hand shading her eyes against the brightness. Shivering suddenly, it seemed to her that the trees darkened, casting long shadows, their branches stretching down towards her. As she stared, she became certain that someone was watching in the forest, someone who didn't want to be seen and her heart raced with fear. She stopped shading her eyes and just as suddenly everything was bright again. 'It's my imagination,' she thought. 'Why would anyone be watching us?'

"Let's fetch the tools from the cottage," Patrick said.

Rosie did as the other two and rested her bike by the whitewashed wall. She followed them into the one-roomed cottage. Although it was mid-July the room was cold. Two small windows let in little light and they left open the top of the half door to lift the shadows. The room was furnished with a small table and some rickety chairs and a cupboard in the alcove beside the fireplace.. Between the windows rested a wheelbarrow and an odd-looking narrow spade, with a long piece of metal jutting out from its base.

While Rosie was wondering about the piece of metal, already Edward was out the door with the wheelbarrow and spade. They followed along a track to where a deep trench had been cut into the bog.

"Now, Rosie," Edward said, taking the narrow spade, "I'll cut the turf with this slean, then heave it up to you. You put each sod into the wheelbarrow and Patrick, you bring it up to the usual place below the trees and spread it out for drying. Later, we'll foot last week's turf. All right?"

Without waiting for an answer, he jumped into the deep trench and set to work, digging, turning, then lifting each sod with the jutting blade and throwing it up to Rosie. The turf was wringing and soon her clothes were soaking. She stacked the wheelbarrow till it was full, then Patrick struggled up the hill. It took him some minutes to spread the load and each time he got back Rosie had a number of sods ready to stack again.

It was backbreaking work for the three of them and they laboured for a couple of hours in silence, concentrating on the task, too tired to talk.

"Time for a cup of tea," Edward announced at last. "Patrick, you know where everything is. Go down to the cottage and boil the kettle. "I'll mark out another trench. Rosie, you take the last barrow up to the trees."

Rosie concentrated on keeping the barrow upright on the narrow track. Her arms were weary and every muscle strained with the effort of pushing the heavy turf. As she neared her goal a gust of wind made the barrow lean to one side. She had great difficulty recovering the balance.

As she set the load down Rosie heard a rustling noise above her. A squirrel or a bird hidden in the branches? The turf was drying in the sunlight, just below the forest shade, yet high enough to catch the mountain breezes. Rosie began to spread the sods, suddenly feeling isolated, friendless. She looked back, but Edward was no longer near the trench and the cottage seemed very far away. Patrick must have lit a fire for she saw wisps of smoke curling from the chimney. The cosiness was all too distant.

The wind whipped up again and the sun dipped behind a cloud. A broad band of shadows swept across her, and spread down the hillside to cover the cottage. The bog seemed like the loneliest place on earth to Rosie and she wanted to run. She wanted to reach the others and feel safe once more.

Overcome by a fear she could not explain, Rosie was about to make a headlong dash when her heart jumped with terror as she found her arm gripped tight and the oily voice of Leonard Reddin murmured, "This is a dangerous place for a young girl. People have disappeared up here and never been found again."

Desperately she tried to free herself.

"No point in struggling," he said, his voice soft. He dragged her towards the trees in spite of her resistance. She opened her mouth to scream but no sound came. For a second she lost her will and went along with Reddin but then, fiercely, she pulled against him. The sudden movement took him by surprise and she jerked herself free. She moved backwards away from him, keeping his every move in sight.

Reddin stared at her and laughed. "Proper heroine, ain't you!" He sneered. "I wasn't going to touch you, you know. Just wanted a bit of privacy."

"Why?" Rosie stopped. "Why did you want privacy?"

He shrugged. "Oh, I was going to show you what could happen to someone who crossed me. Then you could pass the information to your precious friend O'Neill, as a helpful warning. You can still see if you want. I promise, I've no interest in harming you. Wouldn't you like to help your friend?"

Rosie hesitated. After all, she was here to help Edward. That was why she'd come back. But how could she be sure Reddin intended her no harm? His glittering eyes made her shudder. And what was it he wanted her to see? Overcome by a nameless dread, Rosie was unable to move one way or the other and Reddin began to walk towards her.

Down below Edward came out of the cottage. He could barely make out the figure of a girl against the trees and didn't see Reddin at all. Cupping his hands over his mouth he called, *"Rosie! Rosie! Come on down! Tea's nearly ready!"*

He waited.

After a pause, Reddin stepped back into the forest.

Rosie turned and raced towards the cottage. Halfway down the sun came out and the day lit up once more.

Chapter 12

Dried sods of turf were blazing in the hearth and heated the cool room. The kettle was whistling on a brass primus stove. Patrick had covered the old table with a bright plastic cloth from the cupboard and set down a mug and a plate of sandwiches for each of them. He began making the tea while Rosie sat down, trembling.

Edward smiled at her. "Proper tea today," he said. "Maria always saves some for turf days. She thinks we need it after all our hard work." He chatted on, but Rosie could scarcely pay attention, drinking in the sunlight which gleamed through the small windows, the warmth from the fire, the *niceness* of Patrick and Edward.

When Patrick poured the drawn tea and Edward added milk to her cup, Rosie burst out crying. Father and son were dismayed.

"My tea's not that bad," Patrick joked, hoping to cheer her up. She wasn't going to go silly on him, was she? That'd be desperate when they were getting on so well.

Rosie managed a teary smile and then cried louder.

"Oaf!" his father said.

107

"What did I do?" Patrick was hurt.

"You've upset her," Edward said, wishing he had some idea what was wrong.

"No, he hasn't. I'm just – I'm just –" I'm just frightened because Reddin was watching us in the trees and he tried to drag me away, was what she wanted to say but couldn't.

"You're just tired after all the work you've done," Edward said. "And no wonder, since you're not used to it. I should've been more thoughtful." He found a clean hanky in his pocket and handed it to her, looking at her with such concern that she almost wept again.

"Have your tea, Rosie. You'll feel better."

He was right. Gulping the hot liquid she realised how ravenous she was. Eating gave her time to think and she knew there was no point telling Edward about Reddin. For what had Reddin done after all? No harm had come to her and he would deny that he had tried to use force. Telling Edward what had happened would cause worry without achieving anything.

After the food, Edward filled his pipe with tobacco and watched as the colour returned to the girl's face. Really, he was a fool! Rosie came from a world of plenty, where machines did the work and aeroplanes and motors carried them anywhere they wanted to go. How could a girl from a world like that be expected to muck in like the rest of them? There was probably no toiling, no hard labour in 2001. All work could be done by the push of a button. Yet Rosie hadn't complained once, though he could see now how exhausted she was.

"Listen," he said, "I'm going to spread the last of the turf you brought up, Rosie. And there's a bit of footing to do. It will take me maybe an hour. In the meantime Patrick here will keep you company."

"But I'm feeling better now," Rosie said. "I can help."

"Not at all. I'll be quicker on my own, not having to show you how to do the work. And I want Patrick here to look after you, make sure you take things easy."

Rosie had a sudden image of her father's astonishment if he could overhear Edward. 'When it comes to hard labour, Rosie,' he'd often said, 'no one could accuse you of overdoing it. "Take it easy" is your motto.' He'd be gobsmacked at this scene. She grinned at the thought and Edward smiled as he left them. She was looking better already.

As soon as he went, Rosie told Patrick what had happened at the forest. The boy was shocked. "No wonder you were upset. What if Reddin is still up there? He might attack Da – take him by surprise." The boy was filled with foreboding.

"He won't, because then he'd never get his money. He wanted to show me something, as a kind of threat, I think. He said he wanted to show me what could happen if Edward didn't come to the right decision."

They were silent, then Patrick rose abruptly from the table. "I think we should go up there and find out what he meant. We can take another track off the road so that Da won't see us and get back here before him. What do you say?"

In spite of herself, Rosie shivered. What was up there in the forest? She did not want to give words to her worst fears. Yet whatever it was had something to do with Edward. Otherwise Reddin couldn't have used it as a threat against him. Of course they would have to find out.

"Let's go now!" She jumped up, wanting no time to change her mind.

Swiftly they took the road away from the cottage and as soon as it turned a corner and they were no longer in Edward's vision, they cut up to the side of the forest. Out of breath, they stopped. The trees were dense and the bright sunlight made the interior seem even darker.

"Let's work our way just behind the front line of trees, towards where Da is working. Whatever Reddin wanted to show you might be near him."

They moved into the trees and at once had a sense of stepping from day into night. Patrick gripped Rosie's arm, reassuring himself that he had company in this intense blackness. It took a few moments for their eyes to adjust and even then they were overcome by the deep silence and did not move.

"We can't stay here all day," Rosie whispered.

"No. Hang on to my jacket. That way we won't lose each other." The horrifying notion stopped them moving for another minute, then Patrick gathered courage and whispered, "Come on then."

At first they inched forward but as the greenery became more visible they moved faster, careful not to make much noise and talking in whispers. At last they had reached the spot where Reddin had stepped back into the forest. Below, in the sunlight, they could see Edward footing last week's turf into small stacks shaped like miniature wigwams, that would catch the wind and dry from all angles.

"Where do you think Reddin might be?" whispered Patrick.

"I don't know. We'll have to look around."

Looking back into the depths of the forest, their hearts quailed. Neither of them had any doubt but that Reddin was a dangerous enemy. Rosie could still feel his fingers digging into her arm and hear his soft slithery words.

Suddenly Patrick gripped her and she almost screeched with terror. "Look!" he said. "Do you see that?"

He was pointing at a small clearing in the trees, a space not more than twelve feet square. "Whatever he wanted to show you is probably there," he whispered.

"How do you make that out?" Rosie was reluctant to move. She did not want to see.

"Because if he had something to hide, he'd hide it where he could find it again, and this looks like the only place."

He made sense. Rosie took a deep breath, sensing something monstrous in the clearing, something she didn't want to face. She looked back towards Edward, making sure he wouldn't be too far away in an emergency. Her eyes widened and she gulped,

"Patrick, look! The cottage – look!"

The cottage was on fire, flames devouring the thatch as they watched, stunned. Then Rosie saw something else. "Reddin!" she breathed. The man was slipping away from the far side of the blazing building. At the corner of the road he stopped. Was it their imagination, or did he stare straight at them? It wasn't possible, was it? But as they watched, he raised his right arm, fist clenched in victory and they knew the gesture was meant for them. Then he disappeared from sight.

"He was watching every move we made," Rosie said.

"But why set fire to the cottage?" Patrick was still in shock.

111

"To show how far he'll go to get what he wants."

They were riveted to the spot in a kind of trance, knowing they should move, yet incapable, mesmerised by the ferocity of Reddin's deed. How could someone who was prepared to go to such lengths be defeated?

As if in a dream, they saw Edward pause at his work, catch some sound in the air, turn around and shout in horror. Then they saw him racing down, screaming their names, and at last they were galvanised.

"We're safe! We're safe!" Rosie yelled as they rushed after him, but Edward could not hear with the sound of his own terror. He reached the cottage and battled his way through the smoke, but the half-door was in flames and he was beaten back. He surged forward again.

"Da! Stop! We're all right! We're not in there!" Patrick tugged at him.

His father looked at him disbelievingly, then held the boy's head in both his hands, shaking and hugging at the same time.

"That hurts, Da! Stop!" Patrick twisted away. Then his father saw Rosie, touched her face briefly, drew an arm across his eyes and took deep breaths.

In silence he ushered them back from the fire and they watched as the cottage burned to the ground.

Out of nowhere, from other trenches on other hillsides, men, women and children came. They carried anything that would hold water – buckets, pails, cans, kettles – filling them from the stream. For an hour or more they worked until the last of the smouldering embers were soaked and in no danger of setting fire to the mountain and the forest.

"What happened? How did it start?" someone asked after Edward had thanked everyone for their efforts.

"I'm not sure," Edward said. "There was a fire in the hearth. When these two left the cottage one of the sods may have sparked and caught a piece of wood."

Rosie and Patrick found themselves the centre of accusing looks.

"Surely they know better than to leave an open fire?" one man said.

There was nothing they could say. They hadn't after all doused the sods or put a guard up. To tell what they knew would sound as if they were eager to blame someone else. They couldn't prove anything and even if Edward believed them, he could do nothing. So they looked at each other and held their peace.

"Well, I suppose it could've been worse," the same man said. "At least no one was hurt and nothing else caught fire. Imagine if the heather was in flames! And the forest! The whole mountain would be an inferno!"

As they set off for the long journey home, Edward said quietly, "I'll have to let the Turf Board know about the cottage tomorrow. And I hope you two have learned your lesson. I don't know why you left an open fire – just make sure it never, ever happens again."

They cycled in silence, each lost in thought. Edward would never forget those minutes when he believed the two were trapped in the blazing cottage. Patrick brooded on the villainy of Reddin and, with growing anxiety, Rosie wondered how on earth they could save Edward before he was arrested on Thursday.

Edward told his wife about the fire. After that very little was said as they ate the evening meal. Maria put their silence down to shock and exhaustion and showed no surprise when both youngsters opted for an early night.

"We have to talk," Patrick said as they climbed the stairs and Rosie nodded. Once in her room, he burst out, "That man is a lunatic! What are we going to do?"

Rosie had been pondering the same question all the way home and said, "Perhaps Edward could give him the money. Then maybe he won't do whatever it is he's going to do."

"Da won't give him anything!" The boy was definite. "He won't give in to blackmail."

They thought.

"Reddin is coming here tomorrow night," said Rosie. "Maybe we can threaten him with the police."

"It won't work. He'll say he called on Da only to ask for the money he's owed. He'll say he never threatened anyone."

"What about the fire? We saw him."

"We didn't see him start the fire. We've no proof it wasn't our own fault."

They thought again and at last Patrick said, "What about searching his house? We might find something."

"Like what?" Rosie was no longer keen to enter the spider's web.

"Like another letter from Mr Donovan. Or a weapon. Something."

Rosie stared at him so long he became quite uncomfortable. "Maybe it's not such a great idea –"

"It's a terrific idea! It's the best idea ever!"

For a second Patrick felt like a genius. And now that

they had something to do – a definite plan – he was happier.

"How do we get into Reddin's house?" Rosie presumed he had it all worked out.

"Eh – I don't know." Patrick felt he had fallen in her estimation. He was no longer a genius.

"Great. I suppose you think we should knock on his door and say, 'Can we come in, Mr Reddin? We want to search your house for some evidence we can give to the police.'"

"No, I don't." Patrick racked his brain. His brow cleared. "I think we should put a note in his letterbox, saying we saw him set fire to the cottage and we have other witnesses, but we won't go to the police if he leaves Edward alone, and if he wants to talk to us we'll be in the handball alley at twelve noon. That's what I think. – what do you think?"

"That is so clever!" Rosie told him and Patrick, who had never thought much of girls before, basked in her admiration.

Chapter 13

Next morning by eleven o'clock they were standing at the corner of Whitworth Road. A woman with a shopping bag passed by. Some girls played French skipping in the middle of the street and a couple of delivery men with horse-vans made their calls.

No one noticed as Rosie dashed into number 23, posted the note and, almost afraid that Reddin's hand would suddenly emerge from the letterbox to grasp her wrist, rushed back to the corner.

They waited for ages, tormenting themselves with doubts. Perhaps Reddin wasn't in. Perhaps he'd read the note and torn it up. Perhaps he knew they were bluffing about the fire. Rosie wished she had X-ray eyes and could see what was happening inside the house. Not for one moment did they stop watching and eventually their patience paid off.

They stepped behind the corner hedge as the door of number 23 slowly opened. Reddin came out and looked up and down the road, then hurried off in the opposite direction. He was going the right way for the handball alley.

They waited till he'd disappeared then strolled up to the house, not wanting to draw attention. Patrick shoved his hand through the letterbox.

"What are you doing?" Rosie asked.

"Ma always leaves the key on a string inside the door. I thought Reddin might do the same." But it wasn't there and Patrick was bitterly disappointed. "He's such a horrible man," he said. "I mean, everyone leaves the key behind the door or in the lock. But he's so suspicious he doesn't trust anyone."

"No one would do that where I live," Rosie said. "And anyway," she added dryly, "maybe Reddin thinks someone would use the key to search the house behind his back."

"You wait here," Patrick said. "I'll go round the side." Rosie wanted to go with him, but he told her, "You have to keep watch in case someone calls to the house. If that happens, shout through the letterbox, 'Mr Reddin, are you in?' Then the caller won't suspect you're up to anything, but I'll know it's a signal not to make a noise. See?"

Rosie could find no fault with this and once again Patrick looked pleased with himself. He ran down the side passage. Hoisting himself onto the windowsill, he could see the latch on the small kitchen window was broken. Using a copper penny, he managed to inch it open. Then, leaning down, he lifted the handle of the larger window and let himself in.

Rosie studied the front door intently as a man went by. Inside she could hear drawers and presses opening and the louder sound of furniture being dragged around. She prayed the passer-by wouldn't notice. Lost in thought, he didn't even see her. But the next person did. This was a woman who observed everything about her neighbourhood and knew that a caller to number 23 was very rare indeed.

"Are you looking for Mr Reddin, young one?" she asked.

Rosie turned and nodded, wishing she'd go away. From inside came the sound of breaking china. Surely it could be heard all over the road?

Rosie smiled nervously, but the woman merely said, "Well, you won't have long to wait. Here he is now."

"Here who is?" The girl's smile vanished as she saw their enemy at the end of the long road. *"Mr Reddin, Mr Reddin! Are you in?"* she roared through the letterbox. And the noise stopped.

Astounded, the neighbour said, "How could he be in when I'm after tellin' you he's out? He's coming up the road. How can he be in the house? Are you not listenin'?"

"I am." Rosie smiled politely at the woman, craning her neck to see beyond her. The man was still some distance away. She banged on the knocker, rang the bell and roared once more, *"Mr Reddin, are you in?"*

This time Reddin heard her and started running and Rosie gave up all pretence. *"Patrick! Get out! He's coming back!"* She ran.

The boy opened the door and galloped after her down the garden path and up the street.

The woman at the gate stood with her mouth open. "What's going on, Mr Reddin?" She snatched at the man's sleeve as he ran by, but he didn't slow down.

"Mind your own flamin' business!" Snarling, he raced after the other two.

"That's lovely language," she muttered. "That fella has no courtesy whatever. I hope those kids get away."

But Reddin was fit and the distance shortened.

"Rosie," Patrick caught up on her, gasping. "Follow me! Macker lives near here."

He turned down a laneway that led to the backs of some houses. They could hear Reddin pounding behind them.

"Watch me!" Patrick called over his shoulder. Then he veered left through some undergrowth into an overgrown track. Stopping beneath a wall, he hauled himself up. Rosie followed suit and dropped after him into Macker's back garden.

"Over here," the boy pointed to a mound of grass. On the other side of the mound was a small door, shaded by a huge tree. Hastily he opened the door and slid through. Rosie was down on her hunkers when she heard scrabbling at the wall and froze. Patrick pulled her into the air-raid shelter and they stayed still, afraid to close the metal door in case it creaked.

"Where did those flamin' children get to?"

They could hear Reddin and sensed he was looking over the top of the wall.

"*I hope you two are listening, wherever you are!*" he bellowed. "*You're not going to get away with breaking into my house. No one does that to Leonard Reddin. D'you hear?*"

They looked at each other, not daring to breathe. He ranted on, "*You'll pay for this. You think about that fire yesterday and just watch out!*"

Someone came out the back door and marched down the path on the other side of the garden.

"Excuse me, Mister. I'd be obliged if you stopped roaring," a woman said. "We're a respectable family and callers usually come to our front door. They don't hang onto

119

the back wall ranting and raving like lunatics. And if you stay there any longer I'm going to get a policeman!" Her voice was very angry.

"Well, go and get a policeman! I'm not afraid of the bobbies." Reddin was furious. "Get the whole flamin' police force if you want! *Ouch!* What are you doing? You trollop! *Ouch! Aaagh!*"

They heard a crash in the undergrowth. Rosie could not resist peering around the mound. She saw a portly woman holding a rolling-pin, standing at the back wall. There was no sign of Reddin.

The woman addressed the wall. "I'm a respectable married woman and you're a gutty. Calling me a trollop! I will not be roared at by the likes of you! Show your face at the top of my wall again and you'll get your head cracked. Now go on off with you, before I climb over and wallop you into the next world!"

There was a rustling in the undergrowth and the sound of someone moving away. The woman waited a few minutes, then, well satisfied, marched back up the garden path and into the house.

They were in an underground room. Rosie was fascinated, taking in the shelves at the back wall with their canned food, cutlery and delph; the pillows and sleeping bags stacked along one side; the electric light over their heads; the narrow sofa along the other side with its neat pile of old comics. She sat down and picked up a 1938 issue of *The Beano*. "This is brilliant," she said, "but has Macker not got anything more up-to-date?"

"There's a shortage of paper," Patrick was terse, "and we've got more to bother about than comics."

Rosie grinned. "Was that Macker's mother?" she asked. He nodded.

"Then all we have to do is tell her all about Reddin and she'll flatten him." As Patrick frowned, she quickly added, "Just a joke. Lighten up, okay?"

The boy was puzzled. "Lighten up? I'm not an electric bulb, Rosie."

"Will you relax? Reddin's gone. You made an awful lot of noise in his house. What were you doing?"

"I was checking behind the furniture. A vase fell off the sideboard and smashed on the lino."

"When Reddin finds out he'll be in even more of a rage. Did you find anything?"

"I did." Patrick smiled and said no more.

He was very irritating. She held out for a few seconds, then unable to contain her curiosity, burst out, "Well? What did you find? Go on, Patrick. Tell me!"

"I found no proof that he'd anything to do with Mr Donovan's disappearance, but . . ." Annoyingly, he paused again.

"Patrick! If you don't tell me, I'll get really mad!"

"Don't, please. I think you're daft enough already." But he was no longer able to keep it to himself and rushed on, "I found a letter in a wallet under his pillow. Of course I put it back once I read it. It was from a man in England. He wants to meet Reddin tomorrow night about what he calls, 'this extremely serious business'."

"What business? Where's the meeting? Could it have anything to do with Edward?"

"I don't know, but it must be important. And it's a very secret meeting."

"How do you know that?" Rosie was impatient for every bit of information.

"Because it's not in town where other people would be around. They're meeting at 10pm tomorrow night at Boathouse Cove by the cliff walk in Howth. And that must be the loneliest place in the world." His tone was solemn.

Rosie shook away a feeling of dread. "I don't care. We have to be there and hear what they say. It could be really important. Edward's life could depend on it."

Patrick went white. "You don't really think he could be exec – ?" He was unable to say the word.

Rosie too pushed aside the fear. "We've got to make sure we're there tomorrow night. We've got to make sure we do everything to save him."

His face was so tense and strained she felt sorry for him and looked around for some distraction. "I'm hungry," she said. "Can we open some of that tinned fruit?"

"I don't think so," Patrick was reluctant. "Macker's ma put it here in case of an emergency."

Rosie got up and took a can of pears from the shelf. "If you mean an air raid," she said, "I'm not sure, but I don't think there was another one after the North Strand."

"If you're positive?" Patrick was eager to believe her, hunger taking over. "I mean, it'd be a shame if none of those tins were used," he reasoned. "Macker's ma wouldn't want that to happen." Suddenly he felt starving, "I bet if she knew there'd be no more bombing, she'd want us to have a tin. She'd *insist*" Having persuaded himself, he went to the back shelf and got a can-opener.

They sat on the sofa and dipped into the pears. The metal door swung in the breeze, creaking away, but they were too busy eating to bother closing it.

Then they heard a familiar voice. "Who's in our shelter? If it's that lunatic again, I'll batter him!"

Mouths stuffed, they stared at each other. Then, in unison they jumped up and clambered into the sunlight, hidden by the tree from the revenge of Macker's ma, who was once again advancing with her rolling-pin. Any second she would spot them.

Rosie was tempted to run, but Patrick held her back. The woman was marching like a general with a major battle in mind. He pointed to a bush and they inched their way behind it.

Macker's ma did not glance in their direction. She sat down on the grass to lever her way into the shelter. Her face was red with anger, "If I find you in there, I'll pulverise you!" Then she launched herself through the door. As they ran they could hear her bellowing, *"Robber! Gurrier!"*

Once over the wall, they did not stop running till they reached the main road.

Wheezing and gasping, they clutched each other for support.

"We never closed the door of the shelter," Rosie managed at last. "She must have heard it swinging."

Patrick wiped his face with relief. "I'd hate to be caught by her!" he exclaimed. "She's nearly more terrifying than Reddin."

Chapter 14

In the afternoon Maria sat knitting in the garden, different coloured wools in a basket beside her. So far she'd used bright green and red with some yellow. Curious, Rosie sat beside her on the grass, trying to guess what she was making. A scarf, perhaps? A jumper?

"A swimming costume for Patrick," Maria said.

"Swimming togs? In wool? In all different colours?" Rosie had never heard of anything more hideous.

Maria took her shock for admiration. "Yes, indeed. I'm using up all my left-over wool. Look, here's a photo. Isn't it smart?"

She showed a picture of a boy in a pair of light blue bubble-patterned togs. It was beyond Rosie's understanding why anyone would want woolly togs. They'd be very scratchy, plus the sea would make the wool thick and heavy. And imagine sitting on the sand after coming out of the water! Absolute torture! But she couldn't hurt Maria's feelings by saying any of this. Instead she told her, "They look really – eh – different. Really –" she cast around, "really unusual. Yes!"

"Do you think so? Well, I hope Patrick likes the costume as much as you. There's a pattern for girl's togs here as well. Your mother might knit them for you – later on, of course."

Rosie choked, both at the idea of Mum knitting and at the idea of wearing such a revolting pair of togs.

"They're all the rage, you know. And quite easy to do. You might even make them yourself."

Rosie made an excuse and hurried back into the house before Maria got any more bright ideas, like fetching some knitting needles for her.

She had been taught knitting in primary school. "You can't go wrong with a scarf," her teacher, Miss O'Malley, had said, but after some weeks was forced to admit that Rosie could. Her scarf had started off quite narrow and ended up as wide as a small bedspread.

One day an inspector had called and examined Rosie's work with great interest. "I've never seen anything like it," she'd remarked. "I've seen all sorts of knitting. Some with a few faults and some with lots of faults. But how you've managed to get every possible fault into this one piece is beyond me. You've dropped stitches. You've made extra ones. This bit's too loose and that bit is too tight and you've knitted three stitches together here for no apparent reason. I tell you! It's almost a work of genius it's so bad."

The inspector's tone had been awed and Rosie had nearly felt complimented. She knew she would never wear the scarf and was quite chuffed when the inspector asked could she take it "as an example to others".

Her pride had taken a bit of a blow though when Miss O'Malley later explained, rather meanly, that it would an example to others all right – an example of what *not* to do.

After that Rosie gave up knitting. The teacher didn't object and allowed her to read from then on during that class.

When Rosie came in from the garden Patrick was in the dining-room working on his Meccano. The minute he saw Rosie he put the set away and said, "We've got to have a plan for tomorrow night."

"I thought we had one. We just follow Reddin, don't we?"

"Yes, and we probably won't be home before midnight and Da'll kill us. But we definitely can't tell him what's going on because then we won't be let out at all. So what do we do?"

"We'll have to sneak out."

"It's coming home that's difficult. We'll be so late, Da's bound to be waiting up when we get back. We'll be murdered!"

Rosie saw the problem and could think of only one solution. "We must go. And you're right, we can't tell him, so we'll have to put up with all the trouble when we come back. Maybe we'll think of a good excuse for being out so late."

Patrick wasn't a bit happy. "It's all right for you, you'll be gone home soon. But after this I'll be made stay in forever. And Da won't ever stop giving out."

"He will in the end, 'cos we'll have saved him."

"I hope so." Patrick sounded doubtful, but could find no other answer and finally agreed that the following night they'd be waiting near Reddin's house at half past seven and would take their chances afterwards with Edward's anger.

After tea it was still very warm out and Edward was reading

in the back garden. Patrick had gone to give Macker a go on the Rollerblades. "I'll get the gullies from him. Though I'm not telling him we were in his shelter today. If his ma heard I'd be dead. It's depressing. If Da doesn't kill me she will." Poor Patrick was feeling the threat of death from all directions.

Mrs Kennedy had called in for Maria. The two women were off to the pictures. "We're going to see *I Married a Witch*, in the Savoy," Mrs Kennedy said. "Would you like to come with us, Rosie dear?"

"Is it a Roald Dahl film?"

"Never heard of him. It's a Veronica Lake and Frederic March film. Don't you just love her? She's a very glamorous wee lady. And Frederic March has the most romantic moustache you have *ever* seen! Sure you might as well come with us."

Rosie had no interest in romantic moustaches and furthermore had bad memories of the last film she'd seen in the past. "Is it in colour?" she stalled. The neighbour stared at her and she went on hurriedly, "Actually, I won't go, thanks. I've just remembered. I told Patrick I'd wait for him to come back from Macker's."

Mrs Kennedy gave a shriek of delight, "Well now, isn't that lovely, you waiting on your young man? Have you made a wee appointment with him?" She roared laughing and gave Rosie a dig in the ribs.

The girl thought she might kill her. But the woman was on to other things. "Mrs O'Neill dear, I called early 'cos I thought we might do up our legs for the occasion. It'd be more dressy. I brought some Miner's liquid make-up."

Rosie watched what followed with disbelief.

127

Both women wore no stockings, which seemed natural since it was summer. But apparently it was a state which didn't satisfy either of them. Now they set to, putting make-up on their legs to make them look tanned. Then Maria stood while Mrs Kennedy knelt on the floor and drew a black liquid line with a tiny brush down the back of her legs. One line wasn't quite straight and the other was a little smudged, but the neighbour was proud of her effort.

"Dead centre! Now, Rosie," she stood up, "we might be short of silk stockings because of this old war, but wouldn't you think Mrs O'Neill was wearing the best examples you've ever seen?"

"You would," the girl nodded. If you were standing a half a mile away, and had bad eyesight, she thought.

As soon as Maria had done Mrs Kennedy's legs they were off.

"Time for the news," Edward said, a few minutes later. With nothing better to do, Rosie listened to the crackle:

The Allied air raid on Rome was successfully completed on Tuesday night. Warning leaflets were dropped over the city before the raid started. Bombers were asked not to target shrines and other monuments. There were many human casualties but every attempt was made to limit the damage to important sites.

Rosie was shocked, even angry. Why were old statues more important than people? She listened for an explanation, but the newsreader, calm and uninterested, had moved on to the next topic.

The Taoiseach, Mr de Valera has replied to the British Home

Secretary's public criticism of this country's neutrality. He has told Mr Morrison that, while the British fight for the cause of human freedom is to be admired, partition in this country means that the same human freedom has not been given to the Irish people. It is impossible, Mr de Valera implied, to fight side by side with those who deny us the very rights they seem to value so highly when it comes to other countries.

Edward turned off the radio. "Will the people in the North join up with Eire in your time, Rosie?"

"Not by 2001. I think a lot of them want to stay British."

He sighed and was about to ask another question when the doorbell rang. Rosie was glad to answer it. At home she didn't listen much to news about the North. 'I bet I couldn't answer many of his questions,' she thought, suddenly ashamed.

The shock of seeing Leonard Reddin on the doorstep put everything else out of her head. He carried a holdall and was wearing the same thin black gloves as last time. She now remembered that he had not worn them earlier that day. His terrible rage was gone. Now, he was calm, eyes slitted, half-smiling and he seemed even more menacing.

In a panic she went to shut the door in his face but he was too quick and she found his foot jamming it open. He gripped her arm with his free hand.

"Don't you be so hasty, Miss. I haven't come about this morning. After all, no harm done, apart from an old vase and I ain't a spiteful man, am I?" He gave her arm a Chinese burn and Rosie squirmed with pain. "Not spiteful at all," he said softly, his fingers and thumb causing her acute pain. "Lucky I'd forgotten my wallet this morning and had to come back for it," he sneered. "Otherwise who knows what that interfering boy might've found. Too late now though."

Rosie was trying to twist out of his grasp and thought she would shriek with pain when suddenly Reddin let her go.

"It's O'Neill I called to see, not you." He pushed by her and slid down the hall. Rubbing her arm, Rosie followed.

"Ah, Mr O'Neill. I've got something for you." Edward started from his seat, but Reddin waved him back. "Sit down, man. I ain't here to quarrel." Swiftly opening the holdall, he took out a long curved knife. Rosie gasped with alarm and Reddin sliced the air with the weapon, laughed and put it on the table near Edward, then sat opposite him. "Have a look," he said. "You should recognise it."

Edward frowned and picked up the curved dagger, studying the hilt and blade. His expression grew puzzled, "I do recognise it. It belonged to my collection. Just before the war I decided to sell the whole lot. I came to see them as agents of death, not as symbols of adventure and excitement. They were no longer a pleasure. This one I gave to Michael Donovan."

"And he gave it to me when I loaned him that money. Out of gratitude, I suppose. Now I want you to have it back, as a gesture of good will, see. And it's proof along with the letter that I am who I say. It should help you realise what's due to me."

Edward fingered the blade thoughtfully. It was dull and rusty. "When I owned this, I kept it gleaming," he said.

"Yes, well, that's the way it was given to me. Donovan was careless with more than money."

"I gave this to Michael because he thought it was beautiful. It surprises me that he didn't look after it."

"You wouldn't be calling me a liar, would you? I bring

you a gift and you don't believe what I say. That's not mannerly, is it?" Reddin's tone was no longer friendly and Rosie felt afraid.

Edward leaned forward till his face was close to Reddin's. "I want you to understand me very clearly. Michael is a friend of mine. He values gifts. He'd have looked after this one. You obviously had no respect for it." He paused, wanting to be exact, and Reddin stared at him stonily. "You didn't bother to treat this properly and that shows you have no respect for Michael either."

"Why should I respect him? He was a drunkard and a waster and he didn't pay his debts."

"He's an honest man," Edward said quietly. "He'd want to take care of his own debts and when he turns up there's enough money set by for him to do that. But you'll get nothing from me and that's final."

Reddin grew pale. He clenched his gloved fists and for a moment Rosie thought he might lash out at the man facing him. Edward did not flinch or draw back.

"You're a stupid man," Reddin snarled. "When he turns up?" He laughed shortly. "Donovan ain't going to turn up and only a fool would think so!" He was spitting out the words. "You better start figuring out what happened to your friend and partner!"

It was Edward's turn to be shaken. "What do you mean? What happened to him? What are you saying?" And when the man didn't answer he whispered, "What did you do? Are you threatening me now? You know where Donovan is, don't you?"

Reddin stood up, "I know he disappeared. Call that a threat if you want!"

Trying to make sense of his words, Edward said, "Why can't you be straight? You're speaking in riddles."

"No, I ain't. I can see by your face you understand me. Now you best get that money for me by Wednesday night. Otherwise you'll be as unlucky as Donovan."

"Don't threaten me, Reddin or I'll call the police. Rosie here is a witness."

"And you'd put her in danger, would you? I thought not. And you'd best remember that nice family of yours as well. If I were put away, well, I got friends who'd look after my interests."

The two men stared at each other, engaged in a kind of power struggle. Then Reddin shrugged and took up the empty holdall, "I ain't got time for games. Don't bother to see me out. I'll be back Wednesday night. You'd better have that money."

When he was gone, Edward slumped in his chair. "He must have harmed Michael," he said. "What am I going to do, Rosie? If I go to the police, you'll be called as a witness."

"That's okay. I'm not afraid," she lied.

"But it could be months before it came to court. You couldn't stay here that long."

Rosie thought. "I could sign a statement," she said.

"You'd have to come to court. And if you weren't here, God knows what the police would think. Another suspicious disappearance! And even if you came back, there's still the question of Reddin's friends and the danger to Maria and Patrick."

"Do you think he has friends? Maybe he's bluffing."

"I can't take that chance. I can't go to the police. And I can't pay him the money even if I wanted to."

"But you told him it was there."

"It *is* there – in Michael's account – he'd have to sign for it. I can't touch it. And I can't get one thousand pounds by Wednesday. The company is not doing so well and no one is likely to lend me that amount."

Sitting in the gathering dusk, they heard the front door open. Edward seized the knife and put it behind some books in the alcove. "Not a word about this," he said. "I don't want Maria to know anything about Reddin. Promise!"

They listened to Maria's footsteps on the stairs and Edward relaxed a little. "Promise!" he repeated.

"Not to tell Maria? I promise. What are you going to do?"

"I don't know."

"Well, we have till Wednesday to think of something."

He looked at her sternly, his worry increasing. "This is *my* problem, Rosie. You are not to get involved. Reddin is too dangerous for a child to deal with."

Rosie sighed, remembering the adventurous boy Edward had been. He had loved danger then. How had that twelve-year-old become this middle-aged, cautious man?

"If I didn't have to worry about you and the others," Edward sighed, "I'd thrash that villain till he begged for mercy. He'd confess pretty quickly what he's done to Michael."

Remembering how Macker's mother had sent the same villain running, Rosie thought this was a great idea. "Why don't you bash him up?" she said. "I bet he's a coward."

For a second his eyes brightened and Rosie caught a glimpse of the old Edward. "Wouldn't it be wonderful?" Then he grimaced and shook his head. "I'm an adult, Rosie. I can't go around beating up people, even villains. And anyway it might just make him more dangerous. This is one of the worst situations I've ever been in."

"It could be worse," Rosie tried to comfort.

"No, it couldn't. My business partner is missing and that villain hinted at foul play. I'm being threatened. So are you. So is my family. How on earth could it be worse?"

But it will be much worse, she thought. If we don't do something soon, Edward will be arrested for murder and then he'll be executed.

Perhaps there was only one way out, she thought. She could warn Edward and he could make his escape now. He'd have a couple of days to make some plans, then he could clear out, maybe make his way to Switzerland and his brother, Henry.

"Edward –" she began. But then she heard Maria coming downstairs. She entered the room, full of chat about the picture. A few minutes later Patrick was back, showing off the marbles Macker had given him.

With time to think, Rosie reckoned her idea wasn't such a good one anyway. Edward, who worried so much about his family, was not likely to run off on them. He'd see her plan as cowardly.

She and Patrick would have to find another way to save his father's life.

Chapter 15

Tuesday dragged. To make it pass more quickly, they helped Maria clean the house with an enthusiasm she could not understand. It made her suspicious. "Patrick, you hate polishing the floor! Have you done something wrong?"

Her son looked at her sorrowfully. "I just want the place to be nice for Da's birthday," he said.

Maria felt guilty but could not quite believe him. "Mmm. Is there something special you want? Is that why you're so helpful?"

"I want nothing, Ma, except to help you."

Rosie, who was dusting the furniture, thought she might get sick if he kept this up.

His mother felt his forehead. "You're not feeling ill, are you? I mean this isn't your normal behaviour."

"That's not a nice thing to say, Ma." Patrick was enjoying his mother's astonishment.

Maria ran her hand over the top of his head a number of times until he twisted away. "What are you doing, Ma? I can't polish properly."

"I'm trying to feel your halo. My son, Saint Patrick."

"Ma!"

"I ask myself, is this the same boy who doesn't notice that his bedroom is a bombsite? Is this the same boy who runs away from the dishes? Is this the same boy who won't go for a message without moaning and groaning?"

"Ma! I'm a changed person, so I am."

"Oh, go on with you. I give up. You must be up to something. But in the meantime I might as well take advantage. You can clean the cooker after you've done the floor."

"I'm not *that* changed. The cooker is mouldy. Rosie is finished dusting. I'm sure she'd like to do it."

Rosie glared at him, not feeling she had the same freedom to refuse. However, Maria was having none of it.

"Rosie is our guest," she said. "And as such she can't be required to do horrible filthy jobs like scraping out the cooker. No. You can do that while she brings back Mrs Kennedy's make-up for legs."

Behind Maria's back, Rosie made faces, but the boy was too depressed to respond.

Mrs Kennedy was full of the joys of life. "Come in, come in, Rosie dear. Have a glass of milk and some butterballs."

Rosie followed her into the tiny kitchen and sat on a stool while the next-door neighbour poured the milk and took a saucer of butterballs from the press. These were exactly what they sounded like. Butter rolled up into small balls and dipped in sugar.

Rosie looked at them doubtfully but didn't like to be rude. The first one wasn't bad, or even the second, but the third made her mouth greasy and she felt slightly ill. But

Mrs Kennedy wouldn't take no for an answer. "Hasn't every youngster got a sweet tooth, Rosie dear? You must have another. Sure, have the whole lot! If you don't they'll only melt with the day's heat. Now I won't let you leave, Rosie dear, till you've slipped them all down your throat."

The girl gagged. She could only think of the butter turning into a slick yellow liquid in her mouth. Unable to help herself, she stood up and made it to the sink where she retched over and over.

Eyes watering and face beaded with sweat, she stopped at last and looked apologetically at Mrs Kennedy, who was open-mouthed.

"Sorry," she said.

For once the woman was at a loss for words. Rosie ran the water into the sink and tried not to look at the mess she'd made. The neighbour found her voice. "You can leave that, dear."

"I'm so sorry," Rosie said.

"It's not your fault," Mrs Kennedy said distractedly. "That butter must have been off. It must have been rancid – oh dear, oh dear!"

The mention of rotten butter had set Rosie off again and it was a few minutes before she recovered. She wiped her mouth with her hand and said, "Please don't mention the butter again, Mrs Kennedy."

"I won't, love." She took control, armed with Jeyes Fluid and cloths. "Now you just lie down on the sofa in the sitting-room while I clear this."

Gratefully, Rosie did as she was told. The curtains were drawn against the sunlight and as she lay in the half-dark, she thought of Edward and how tragedy was closing in on him. The idea of following Reddin made her ill and she realised that it wasn't so much Mrs Kennedy's butterballs that turned her stomach, but the fear and tension caused by Reddin.

Mrs Kennedy was killed apologising for nearly poisoning her. She came into the sitting-room with a basin of warm water, a face cloth and a towel and, while Rosie cleaned herself, the poor woman said, "I'll never forgive myself. Now, I'll not mention rancid butter again, but I should have known there was something wrong with it. You could be dead, you know. I've never seen anyone get so sick. You should have seen the sink!"

Rosie said she had to go, and ran back home. But Mrs Kennedy followed, insisting on explaining to Maria and Patrick what she'd done to Rosie and going into such details over the girl's performance at the sink that both of them in turn felt quite ill.

Rosie had to excuse herself and go to bed.

In the end what stopped Mrs Kennedy's flow was the sudden realisation that Patrick was looking very odd.

"God bless us, Mrs O'Neill. What happened to him?"

"He was cleaning the cooker." Maria sounded bitter.

"Oh dear, oh dear! Did it blow up in your face, son?"

Maria answered. "No. Patrick took all the dirt, grime and grease out of the cooker, then spread half of it around the kitchen and the other half over himself."

Both women stared at the boy. His face was streaked black and his hair stood on end. His hands and clothes and even his knees were filthy.

"Dear me," said Mrs Kennedy, "you'd think he worked in a coal yard."

Patrick was fed up. He had tried his best to clean the

cooker and what was his reward? Insults and mockery! Now Ma would make him spend the rest of the day at the job. She was a stickler for doing things properly.

Mrs Kennedy saw his misery and came to the rescue. "Now, Mrs O'Neill dear, let me help. After all I'm responsible for that wee girl's illness and I'd like to feel I could do some good today. And sure anybody knows a young fellow like Patrick is useless with a cooker. You may as well have employed an elephant. But you and me now, we'd have it all cleaned in a jiffy!"

Maria was torn between these obvious truths and the desire to make Patrick do the job properly.

Reading her mind, Mrs Kennedy added, "Sure, don't you know he'll only make it all worse? He'll go spreading dirt everywhere. Grease on your walls, grime on your floors, every surface filthy!"

"I suppose you're right," said Maria.

That was the signal for Mrs Kennedy to march down the hall, winking at Patrick who winked back, his relief greater than any resentment he may have felt at being compared to an elephant.

Rosie slept undisturbed until four o'clock. When she woke she felt fresh and contented, until she remembered. A sense of dread engulfed her.

Maria arrived up with a cup of weak tea and a few Marietta biscuits. Plumping up the pillows behind her, she told Rosie to take it easy, stay in bed until she called her for tea. Patrick had gone to get some messages.

"Is he all right?" Rosie said. "He looked desperate this morning."

"Not half as desperate as the kitchen. But everything's back in order now, thanks to Mrs Kennedy. The poor woman is very sorry for nearly killing you."

Rosie giggled, "I think I made more of a mess in her kitchen than Patrick did in yours."

"Impossible! It was like a bombsite after him."

As Rosie sipped her hot tea and ate the biscuits, she felt better, determined now to defeat Reddin. She knew Patrick would not give up either. He was a good friend to have in times of trouble, never short of ideas and he had plenty of courage. Together they made a good team and no matter what it took they would not let Reddin destroy Edward.

As Patrick had foreseen, they'd no problem getting out of the house after tea. In fact, it was Maria who made the suggestion, "Rosie, you look a little pale. What about a bit of fresh air? Why don't you and Patrick take yourselves off for a while?"

"Will I do the dishes first, Ma?" Afraid his mother was still angry, Patrick was anxious to make up for his spectacular efforts with the cooker.

Maria spoke with unexpected force, "I don't want you near my kitchen again today, Patrick O'Neill, so go on out, the pair of you."

They cycled down to Whitworth Road and were just in time to see Reddin come out of his gate and get up on his own bike.

"Great!" said Patrick. "I knew he'd cycle. The buses stop at nine o'clock. He'll be dead easy to follow now."

And so it proved. Reddin had no idea anyone was aware of his plans and he did not look around. Even if he had, he might not have seen them there were so many cyclists on the road.

They followed him into town, down Abbey Street, past the railway station and out beyond Fairview to the coast road. By the time he took the turn for the cliff walk at Sutton Cross, Rosie was feeling exhausted. Not particularly fond of exercise, she was suffering from an overdose. In the last few days she had walked, cycled, spread manure, hauled turf and dusted furniture. It was more than enough to last a lifetime and she hoped it would end soon!

On the last mile of the journey they were the only three on the road, but Reddin never thought to look around. It was dusk when he reached the beginning of the cliff walk. The boy and girl stopped some distance away while he leaned his bike against a wall and put his bicycle clips in his pocket. As soon as he disappeared along the track they parked their own bikes and followed.

Within seconds they could see him clearly as he passed the Martello tower, the sea breaking far below on the rocks. As twilight turned to night, the full moon lit up the ocean and the cliffs and the rocky hillside. They hurried after him and any noise they made was lost in the sound of the waves.

As Patrick had said, it was the loneliest place in the world. A person could fall to their death here, Rosie imagined, and who would ever know what happened? It was the place for a perfect murder. If there were no witnesses, how could it ever be proved whether a person slipped or was pushed? Unbidden the thought came, 'Was Michael Donovan pushed? Is that what happened to him?'

Watching the hunched figure of Leonard Reddin silhouetted against the moonlight, his face hidden by the jacket collar he had pulled up, she found it easy to believe he was a murderer. She found it easy to believe too, looking at the waves sucking away from the rocks beneath, that a body could be carried far out to sea and never found.

The path narrowed and they had to walk in single file. They froze when Reddin half-turned, but he was just making sure of his grip as he edged across a difficult piece of cliff face where the track narrowed to a foot's width.

Patrick followed confidently, but Rosie was more nervous. Her fingers scrabbled at the rocks and when she lost her grip and swayed, she could not help crying out. Patrick grabbed her arm and they were motionless. Ahead, Reddin stopped and listened. He turned around and they pressed their faces against the wall of rock, praying. If he saw them, they were trapped. Rosie knew that with awful certainty. She could not run away here. If she tried she'd fall to her death.

But if Reddin noticed two shapes he took them to be part of the cliff and soon he was on his way again.

The rest of the track to Boathouse Cove was easier and, when the man took the downward path, Rosie and Patrick watched from above, lying flat on a grassy patch which was yellow and gold in the moonlight.

They saw him unlock the boathouse and enter. Patrick's imagination worked overtime. "Maybe Mr Donovan is a prisoner in there," he whispered.

"But he disappeared a year ago," Rosie said. "He's hardly been a prisoner for that long. Somebody was bound to come by and find him."

"Maybe." Patrick didn't want to give up his theory. It would be nice to rescue Michael Donovan and clear up the mystery so simply.

But it was obvious there was no prisoner in the boathouse when Reddin emerged leaving the door open. He was carrying a lighted lantern and climbed to a low-lying rock. Then he swung the lantern a number of times, signalling out to sea. In the distance they saw an answering signal.

"It's from a fishing trawler, " Rosie said. "What's going on?"

Reddin set the lantern down where it was visible to anyone watching from the trawler. Then he waited on the small jetty, sheltered by the overhanging cliff.

Soon enough they heard the splash of oars as a large rowboat came into view. The single oarsman threw a line to Reddin who hauled him in and tied the rope to an iron ring.

Silently the two went to the boathouse and came out carrying boxes, stacking them neatly and efficiently in the boat. When it was full the man set out for the trawler. He made three such trips, until the boathouse was empty. Not a word was spoken by either man apart from grunts of exertion. It was a routine they must have followed many times.

On the clifftop, Rosie waited. Was this all that was going to happen?

"It's a smuggling racket," Patrick told her.

"I'd never have guessed," Rosie was withering. "But it doesn't tell us anything about Michael Donovan and what happened to him."

Then, as the man rowed in for the last time, he called cheerily, "All that tea and butter should make good money. Where'd you get it this time, mate?" His accent was English.

"From a warehouse on the quays. The watchman owes me a favour. Which reminds me, so do you!"

143

Neither man made any attempt to keep his voice down and the words carried clearly on the night air to the watchers above.

"Do I? I thought we was doing each other a favour. You get the goods. I sell 'em on. We split the profits fifty-fifty. Equal partners, mate. No favours owing."

Now Reddin's voice became a snarl. "Listen, Wilson. If I hadn't let you in on this black-market racket, you wouldn't be so well off, would you? You wouldn't be able to give that kid of yours the delicacies and care she needs, would you? I bet her medical treatment is expensive!"

"So what if it is? I don't begrudge her!" Wilson was defiant.

"You won't want to lose this source of income then, will you? Trawlermen like you are ten a penny. I could replace you tomorrow."

He let the threat hang in the air and when the Englishman next spoke he was no longer cocky, but anxious and subdued. "What favour do you want?"

"I have a chance of owning one third, maybe more, of a company called *Donovan O'Neill*. It's an import/export business. With its licence we could use half the goods they bring in to sell on to the black-market in England. We'd make far more than we do now with these few boxes- a fortune beyond your dreams."

"I never expected to make this much, Reddin. It does me."

Reddin swung around and seized the other man by his shirt front. "It doesn't do me!" he spat. "I aim to be rich and you won't be a part of any of it if you don't help me!"

Shaken, the man said, "Calm down, mate. Did I say I wouldn't help? What is it you want me to do?"

"Once I own one third of *Donovan O'Neill*, I need to take charge of the business. Edward O'Neill has no vision, see? He won't play the black market. Fancies himself as an honest man. A fool is what I'd call him! He must be got rid of, so I can get control."

The words were cold, full of menace. Patrick shuddered and Rosie closed her eyes in dread. They were not the only ones who felt afraid.

"You mean to kill him!" Wilson's voice was hoarse. "I don't see how that –"

"Not kill him, you fool! Get him arrested for the murder of his partner, Donovan, who disappeared last year. A most convenient event." He laughed as if this were a great joke, but Wilson was silent. After a moment Reddin went on, "If he's convicted for murder, then I can forge a will, entitling me to what Donovan owned. With O'Neill out of the way and his brother in Switzerland, I'd be in charge. What I want you to do is say you saw him murder Donovan in the Dublin Mountains one year ago. I'll give you the exact time and place. You can say you didn't come forward sooner out of fear. But now your conscience is at you. Say –"

"You murdered him, didn't you? Now you want me to commit the same crime. O'Neill will be hanged. I'll have no part in that!" Wilson was visibly shaking, his voice trembling with horror. Reddin said nothing, not looking now at the other man, but out to sea, calculating his next move. On the clifftop the two friends hardly dared to breathe in case they missed any of the drama unfolding below.

"Pity," Reddin spoke at last, his voice calm and conversational as if he were discussing the weather. "We could be rich. You're making a big mistake. The mistake of

145

a lifetime, I'd say. I hear old Churchill doesn't approve of the black market. He doesn't approve of villains like you trying to fleece your own people. You could spend a few years in prison if this got to the wrong ears. Then what would your little girl do? Mother dead, no relatives, father in prison. She wouldn't last long in a home, a delicate kid like her –"

"Shut up! You needn't go on. I'll do what you want."

"Right. Call to my house tomorrow morning. I'll give you the details then. That gives you a few hours to be certain you're with me. Of course, if you're not – well, you know the score. I'm afraid it'll be a few days before you can take the trawler back to England."

Wilson turned away and made for his boat.

Rosie and Patrick inched back from the edge, rose and hurried back along the cliff walk. They said nothing for a long time, each grappling with the enormity of Reddin's evil plan.

On the long cycle home, they pondered.

It was Rosie who spoke first. "Even if Reddin gets the thousand pounds, he'll still try to destroy your father."

Patrick agreed. "He wants the money, but he wants to take over the company too."

They decided to tell Edward everything. "Then the police can arrest Reddin." Patrick was confident. "We'll be witnesses to what he said. That will be proof that he's a murderer."

Rosie wasn't so sure. Reddin and Wilson would deny their conversation. It would be the men's word against theirs. And it would be a bit tricky for her to be a witness in court. She had to go home on Friday, otherwise Mum and

Dad would be in a panic. Even if she were to come back, any trial could take months and she could hardly find an excuse to be away so long. All of her visits to the past had been a week or less and Rosie knew instinctively that any longer would be impossible.

But Patrick was in such good form at the notion of stopping Reddin that she hadn't the heart to explain the difficulties.

"I agree we should tell Edward," was all she said in the end. "Then at least he'll be warned."

She felt drained and exhausted, but Patrick whistled with happiness. "Da can have a great birthday now," he said.

"How will he feel when he hears Michael Donovan was murdered? He keeps thinking he'll turn up."

The boy hadn't thought of this and his spirits dropped. "He is fond of Mr Donovan," he said. Then his heart lifted defiantly, "When we tell the police what we heard, they'll know who to arrest. That's good, isn't it? And when we tell Da, he won't be wondering any more what happened to his old friend. Everything will be clear. He won't be happy, but at least he'll know for certain. That has to be good too."

Chapter 16

But when they got home Edward gave them no chance to explain anything. It was long after midnight and as soon as he heard the gate swing open he was out on the front step, grim and furious.

"Where were you?" He addressed Patrick but gave him no opportunity to answer, all his pent-up worry spilling over. "I've been up and down Griffith Avenue any number of times over the last three hours. I called in to your friend Macker. I went to Johnno's. I looked in at the handball alley. But there was no sign anywhere of either of you! Where did you get to?"

Patrick opened his mouth but got no chance to reply, his father bursting out, "You've no idea of the worry you caused. Where on earth did you get to? Have neither of you any sense of responsibility? To disappear like that!"

"We went to –" Rosie started, but Edward wasn't listening.

"Luckily your mother doesn't know you were missing. She came back from a visit to Mrs Doyle's at eleven o'clock, and went to bed thinking the two of you were already safely asleep. I didn't have the heart to tell her otherwise. All the worry you've caused! Both of you."

"But Edward –" Rosie got no farther. He reminded her of Mum and Dad. When they got annoyed, *really* annoyed, they couldn't or wouldn't listen till they'd calmed down. Now Edward, who had just demanded explanations, waved a hand at her, still incensed. "I don't want to hear any excuses tonight. Not a word! It's far too late. Put up the bikes and get yourselves to bed as quietly as mice. Not a sound. I don't want your mother wakened."

As they wheeled the bikes round the back he called after them, "Don't think this is finished. I want a full account of your atrocious behaviour tomorrow. And you'd better have good reason for it. And you, Patrick, you needn't expect to be allowed out gallivanting again for quite some time."

"Oh well," Rosie thought as she tiptoed up to bed, "we can tell him in the morning. Maybe he'll listen then."

But next morning Rosie slept till midday. When she got up Edward had long gone. Patrick came downstairs even later. "Why didn't you wake me early, Ma?" he complained.

Maria was astonished. "Is there no end to life's surprises?" she said. "Yesterday you wanted to help clean the house and today you want to rise with the lark! This is not the Patrick I know. I thought you'd love a lie-in."

"Will Da be home for his dinner?" he asked, not responding to her mockery.

"No, son. He won't be home till this evening. He's got a lot of orders to get out."

Mrs Kennedy, who had the knack of hearing things first, found out in the afternoon that *Pay an' Take* had got in a consignment of flour and she and Maria and most of the neighbourhood women rushed down to join the queue.

The day was snailing along for the two friends.

Macker and Johnno called and for a while they played rounders in the back garden, using a tree-trunk as a wicket. Rosie was quite good at batting and useless at bowling. A few times Macker went to sneer, but changed his mind, remembering the Rollerblades and how he'd like to try them again.

Then they played *Three an' In*, she and Patrick against the other two. It was a kind of soccer played with any ball available, in this case an old tennis ball. Briefly, Rosie wished she'd brought back a proper football. Macker's eye would have been properly wiped.

For a while she found it almost impossible to connect her foot with the tennis ball, but then she got the hang of it and scored one goal to Patrick's two.

At the end, Macker whacked her and said, "You're not bad!" and Rosie whacked him back saying, "I'm better than you. You didn't score any goals."

When the other boys had gone, Patrick tried to fill in the time till his father's return by teaching Rosie *Jackstones*, played with five small stones he picked from the flowerbed. He told her the rules: there were six steps and each step started by throwing all the stones a small distance in the air.

1. Fives: Catch all five together on the back of the hand.

2. Fours: Let the five stones fall to the ground, take any one as the Jackstone, throw it up and while it's in the air, pick up the other four in one go, catching the Jackstone as it comes down.

If the stones are too far away from each other to pick up,

150

the player can throw the Jack into the air and edge the stones closer together before catching the Jack. As long as the Jack doesn't fall on the ground, this can be done any number of times until the stones are close enough to pick up in one go.

3. *Threes plus One:* Let all five fall to the ground. Select and throw the Jack and pick up one stone. Throw up the Jack again and pick up three together (not forgetting to catch the Jack each time.).

4.*Twos.* Let all five fall to the ground. Throw up the Jack, pick up two stones and catch the Jack on the way down. Do the same with the other pair of stones.

5. *Ones.* Let all five fall to the ground. Throw the Jack and pick up a stone before catching the jack. Repeat three more times.

The person who could do all of this successfully won the game.

Rosie made a hames of it. The stones would not fall on the back of her hand. They scattered on the ground. She could not get beyond the first step and what she'd thought was a simple, unsophisticated game turned out to be quite difficult. But her hopelessness made them both smile and kept them distracted for a while.

But in the end there were no more games they wanted to play.

Time crawled while they waited for Edward. Rosie thought how odd it was that the hours moved so slowly and yet they had so little time left to rescue Edward. Tomorrow was the 19th of July and that was the date of the newspaper Rosie had found in the junk shop. Whatever was to happen would happen in the next twenty-four hours. Looking ahead those hours seemed an eternity. "Will they never pass?" Rosie agonised.

But events, when they began to move, moved very quickly.

Maria was in great form when she came back. The shopping expedition had been successful and, as she made the tea, she danced around the kitchen singing '*Jealousy*'. When her son looked into the kitchen she tried to make him do the tango.

"Ma!" he said indignantly as she seized him.

'My *pride was in my jealous*y,' chorused Maria, hauling her son around. She gave up almost immediately and he made good his escape while she shouted after him, "I might as well be dancing with a sack of potatoes!"

Within half an hour they were eating and still Edward was not home. "Your poor father's still working," Maria said. At that moment the doorbell rang. "Perhaps that's him. He may have forgotten his key." She went out and they heard the murmur of conversation in the hall.

"It's a man to see him," she said, coming back shortly. "A Mr Reddin. I've put him in the sitting-room. He's not a very friendly type – won't even take a cup of tea."

Patrick and Rosie looked at each other in consternation. With one accord they rose, but before they could see the visitor, the front door opened and Edward was home at last.

"Da!" Patrick rushed out.

"Edward!" Rosie followed.

"Let him catch his breath," Maria laughed, close on their heels.

"We have to speak to him!" they said in unison.

"Whatever it is can wait till he sees his visitor. He's in the sitting-room." Maria took her coat from the hall stand. "Now, I'm just going over to Mrs Doyle to make her some tea and keep her company. You look after your father, Patrick. I'll be back in an hour." She kissed Edward's cheek and was gone.

"What visitor?" Edward opened the sitting-room door and the other two pushed in after him.

Reddin had made himself at home, sitting comfortably in an armchair, legs stretched out, ungloved hands drumming on the sides in time to a tune he was humming.

Edward wasted no time. "Listen, Reddin, I'm not giving you any money. I don't have available cash, but even if I did, you wouldn't get it. So, there's no point in your calling here any more. I consider you an out-and-out villain and I want you to leave my house at once. You're not to bother us any more. Is that plain enough for you?"

Reddin's smiled. "Very plain, but I'm afraid it won't do. I've given you every opportunity to pay what I'm owed. And your refusal means you're going to be bothered a great deal!"

He didn't rise from his chair and showed no intention of moving.

"If you don't leave, then I'll call the police," Edward said, his fists clenched.

"Oh, I'll leave all right, but I've got a few things to say first." As Edward started to object, he added, "I accept you won't pay me, so now just listen, right!"

"As long as you're quick," Edward said tersely. He sat on the edge of a chair and the other two stood behind him.

Reddin took his time, leaning forward slightly and folding his arms. "I know someone who saw what you did to Donovan," he said.

Edward was bewildered. "What are you talking about?"

"There was a day last summer when you and Donovan were cutting turf in Glencree," said Reddin.

"There were many such days." Edward was impatient, but the other man ignored this interruption and began to paint an elaborate scene. "And my friend, who was on a holiday in the area, was out walking."

"Is there any point to this rigmarole?" Edward was peppering.

"It was warm and the midday sun got too hot for my friend, so he sat in the shade of the forest for a while and fell asleep."

"Really?" Edward tried sarcasm. "Your friend's holiday sounds riveting, but I can't see what it has to do with me."

"If you'd shut up and listen, you would see. My friend was woken by shouts – screams more like. What does he hear except Donovan pleading, 'Don't, Eddie! Don't!' According to my friend those were the very words. And then he hears more terror and more pain. Naturally, he has a look, cautious-like because he doesn't want to get involved in violence. And what does he see?"

Drawn into the tale at last, Edward asked with awful fascination, "What did he see?"

"He saw you, standing over Donovan's bloodied body. He saw you drag him into the trees and he watched while you dug his grave and buried him in that lonely place. That's what he saw."

As the three stared, mesmerised, he repeated softly, "That's what he saw."

Speechless, they grappled with the scene. But Reddin wasn't finished. Sitting back again, he said conversationally, "I expect you're wondering why you did it, O'Neill? Well, everyone knows Donovan had debts, that he wanted to take money out of the company, that there were arguments, that he drank too much and spent more time in *The Cat and Cage* than at work. Everybody knows how much better off your business would be without him. No wonder you got fed up and murdered him!"

Edward was so shocked he was unable to defend himself. But Patrick and Rosie spoke at once.

"Liar!"

"We know you set this up!"

"We heard you last night in Howth!"

Reddin paled, but swiftly recovered. "You can't prove a thing. You're family and the police will say you're covering for him. My friend will stick to his story. Anyway there's too much proof!"

But now Edward had grasped the full significance of Reddin's tale. His expression changed from horror to sadness and then to fury. Jumping to his feet he lifted Reddin from his chair.

"You piece of slime! So that's what you did to my old friend. You're a coward and a louse!" He shook Reddin as if he were a dishrag and the man almost choked with fright. Freeing himself, he stumbled out of the room and opened the front door, squealing back, "You had your chance. Now you can wait for the hangman's rope!"

Edward went after him but he scurried away like a rat.

Chapter 17

When the villain was gone, Edward collapsed into a chair, totally stunned. He wanted to believe the last half hour was a nightmare from which he would soon awaken. Could anyone be as evil as the man who had just left? And what he'd said was insane, wasn't it? He looked to his son and Rosie for some comfort, but their account of all that had happened gave him none.

It took them more than an hour to fill in the details but this time Edward listened attentively, making no comment even when they told him about breaking and entering and of their adventures the previous night and of the hold Reddin had over the Englishman.

When at last they were finished, he sat quietly, shaking his head, saying, "It would seem that poor Michael Donovan is dead, God rest his soul. And if Reddin's twisted words are in any way true, then he met an awful death. In spite of what that villain says, I never wanted him to come to harm, but hoped one day he'd get better. I wished him well, nothing else."

Rosie was embarrassed by his need to explain and Patrick

said quickly, "We know that, Da. You don't have to say it."

Rosie, anxious for his safety, added, "I don't think you should stay here, Edward. You'll be arrested for murder."

He looked at her, shocked, "Surely you don't believe I murdered –"

"No, I don't. But the reason I came back was because I read about your arrest in tomorrow's papers – it's all right, Patrick knows – you'll be charged with murder if you don't leave. One way of changing your future is not to stay here!"

"I can't run away, Rosie!"

"You can. At least until we sort out Reddin."

And Patrick urged, "Please, Da, do as she says!"

But his father shook his head. "Two thirteen-year-olds can't resolve this. No. I've made up my mind. I'll go to the police, tell them everything. They'll sort it out. It's their job."

Haunted by the newspaper report, Rosie would have tried again, but once more the doorbell rang and Patrick answered it. He returned, followed by two men in uniform. Rosie's heart sank.

"Mr O'Neill, sir?" asked the sergeant.

Edward nodded and the sergeant showed him an official-looking document. "I have a warrant to search the premises. You may accompany me while I do so. Garda Finnegan will stay here with these two youngsters."

They left the room. Listening in silence the others could hear drawers and presses being opened. After what seemed ages, they returned, the sergeant holding Michael Donovan's note to Reddin.

"I keep telling him that wasn't sent to me," Edward was pale, "but he doesn't believe me."

"I would point out, sir, that this note was in your drawer, in your possession."

"It doesn't mention my name. It was sent to Reddin!"

"Mr Reddin told us you might say that. It doesn't mention his name either, sir. Of course if it belongs to him then that will be clear when it is examined for fingerprints. Now, I'd like to search this room, sir."

In a blinding flash, Rosie knew the reason for Reddin's gloves on his earlier visits. He must have cleaned his fingerprints from the note – and the dagger. Only Edward's prints would be found. And she could see from the expression of the others that the same truth had dawned on them.

From behind the books on the shelves, the sergeant drew out the dagger.

"What have you been hiding here, sir?" He sounded triumphant.

"I haven't been hiding anything! Except from my wife, that is." Edward stopped, realising from the policeman's glance how badly this sounded.

"Mmmm. Now what would you say this is?" He was examining the blade.

"Rust," said Rosie.

"Oh, I think you'll find that's not accurate, Miss. I think you'll find these marks here are bloodstains. And what does that tell you?"

They waited while he turned the blade, peering closely. "That tells you this could be the murder weapon."

"My father's not a murderer!" Patrick's voice was shaking.

The sergeant seemed to change the subject. "Solving a

crime can be very interesting," he told them. "It's like fitting the pieces of a jigsaw together. In this case we've already got some of those pieces. We have the note which gives us a motive. We have the knife, which upon scientific examination may show bloodstains and could therefore be the murder weapon. And we may have fingerprints. But we are missing one major piece. Now, what do you think that could be?"

Edward, who did not like his old friend being referred to as a major piece in a jigsaw puzzle, nevertheless hid his distaste and said, "I suppose you're referring to the body."

"Indeed, sir! Correct, sir. And of course there is one other lesser piece which will lead us to that major find. Any ideas?"

Since no one said a word this time, he supplied the answer himself. "A witness is what we need. And according to Mr Reddin we have one. The man will give his statement later tonight, when he is finished his day's fishing and brings in his trawler. In the meantime he has told Mr Reddin all he knows and he in turn has told us. So we are well informed as to the whereabouts of the body and you, sir, will accompany us to recover it."

Edward shuddered and the sergeant looked at him with satisfaction, taking his reaction for guilt and fear. Then he clicked his heels, stood to attention and said, "Edward O'Neill, I am arresting you for the murder of one Michael O'Donovan. You do not have to say anything but I must warn you that anything you do say will be taken down and may be used as evidence against you. Do you understand?"

"I didn't harm Michael," Edward answered. "You're making a mistake."

But the garda had moved forward and now he handcuffed Edward's left wrist to his own right one. Without further protest, Edward went with them, only turning to say, "Patrick, tell your mother what's happened. Do it gently."

Mrs Kennedy had heard the police car and was in her garden when Edward was escorted out. Astounded, she put a hand to her forehead and called out, "Mr O'Neill, what's happening?"

Distracted with worry, it was Patrick who told her, "They're arresting him for murder!"

"Don't be daft!" The woman said, but saw by his face that it was true. "It's a silly joke!" She addressed the sergeant, "You should have more to do with your time than be tormentin' respectable citizens with charges of murder. Sure the lord knows that man couldn't murder a hen!"

The sergeant smiled, "We're not arresting him for murdering a hen, madam. Murdering hens is not a crime, unless the aforesaid poultry belongs to someone else, in which case the crime is one of larceny and malicious damage."

Mrs Kennedy lost her rag. "Did I ask for a lecture on hens?" she shouted. "This is typical! When someone objects to a law-abiding neighbour being arrested for murder, what do they get? A silly lecture on hens."

"You will get something else, madam!" muttered the sergeant. "You will get arrested for disturbing the peace."

There was a further distraction at the gate, where a fellow stood taking photographs of the whole proceedings. Reddin must have told a reporter, Rosie thought. The policeman led Edward into a black car. The sergeant sat in beside the driver and told the two youngsters, "Any enquiries about Mr O'Neill can be made at Whitehall Garda Station." Then the car moved off, Edward staring straight ahead.

"Where's your poor mother?" Mrs Kennedy asked.

"In Mrs Doyle's."

"Do you want me to fetch her?"

Patrick nodded. "Will you tell her what's happened? Please."

"Of course I will, son. I'll tell her nice and easy."

Patrick and Rosie went back inside.

"We have to move fast before your mother comes back," Rosie said. "Let's go over everything since Reddin called. We might find something that will help us."

They teased through all they could remember. It was when Patrick mentioned *The Cat and Cage* where Donovan drank that Rosie remembered something.

"That's it. That's it!'

"What is?"

"Michael Donovan told Edward his journal was with a cat behind bars. Edward thought it was a silly joke. He hadn't got a cat and who would keep one behind bars anyway? But he must have meant *The Cat and Cage* pub in Drumcondra!"

"But if he left it in the pub," Patrick said slowly, not wanting to let his hopes rise in case they were dashed again, "do you think it could still be there?"

Rosie was already up halfway up the hall. "We won't find out sitting here!"

"Wait! I'll just leave a note for Ma, telling her we'll be back soon." He found a sheet of paper and quickly scribbled. Then the two were out the door and running.

It seemed to take forever to reach *The Cat and Cage*, but it could not have been much more than ten minutes. They arrived gasping and Patrick said, "I think Mr Donovan drank in the upstairs bar. I was with Da once when he met him here."

They rushed upstairs. Some customers were sitting at small tables, but no one was at the bar.

Rosie got straight to the point, asking the middle-aged barman, "Do you know anything about Mr Michael Donovan's journal? Please. It's so important."

He studied them for a minute, cleared some glasses from the counter and said coolly, "I might. But then again, I might not."

"Please, Mister. If you have it, you've got to give it to us." Patrick was pleading.

"Oh, and I suppose it's a matter of life and death." The barman said sarcastically.

"Well, yes, it is actually," Rosie told him. "That's it exactly!"

The man raised an eyebrow, "Bit dramatic, aren't you?" But he noted how anxious they were. The boy's face was shiny with sweat and the girl looked weary. After a moment he said gently, "Listen, Mr Donovan gave me a suitcase to look after. It's locked, which seemed funny at first, because it was so light I thought it was empty. But then I could hear something sliding around when I was carrying it. That could be your journal."

"Will you give us the suitcase then, so we can see?" Patrick tried to find the right persuasive words. "I promise you, we're not being dramatic. We want the journal for a good reason!"

The barman hesitated, half-convinced, then shook his

head. "Mr Donovan said I was to give it to one particular gentleman and no other. I promised not to part with it to anyone else."

"Oh God!" Rosie felt she would go mad. "You won't listen, will you? We need that journal! This is stupid. Nobody else has turned up to collect your precious suitcase, so why don't you just, *please*, give it to us!"

The barman bristled. Here he was trying to be nice and explain matters and what did he get for his efforts? Insults, that's what! Stupid, was he? The nerve of her! Kids these days had no manners.

"You could do with a bit of politeness," he told Rosie. "It's not me who doesn't listen. I told you. I gave my promise. Mr Donovan was a valued customer and I liked him. He treated me like a friend. I don't know what happened to him, but the least I can do is keep the promise I made. There's no more to be said on the matter. Now it's not my job to deal with cheeky kids, so you can take yourselves off the premises. Pronto." He sniffed.

Dejected, they turned away but Rosie, feeling a bit ashamed of herself, turned back to the barman and sighed, "Sorry, Mister. I didn't mean you were stupid exactly. I just got carried away 'cos nothing we said made any difference."

She saw his face soften and pushed her luck one last time, "Are you sure you can't give us the case? I know you made a solemn promise, but if the person you're holding it for never came to pick it up, there's no point –"

Before she could finish, Patrick had a brainwave and interrupted, "Was it Mr O'Neill you said you'd give the case to?"

"It was!" The man was curious now. "How did you know that?"

"It was a guess. Mr O'Neill was his friend too. He's my father. I can prove it, well nearly. Look."

Patrick took an old library ticket from the pocket of his shorts and the barman scrutinised it. "Your name is O'Neill all right and your address is in Griffith Avenue which is what Mr Donovan said. Why didn't Mr O'Neill collect the case himself?"

"He didn't know it was here. We only found out today where the journal might be. My father can't collect it now because he's – he's –" Patrick stopped, suspecting the barman would never hand over the case if he knew his father was charged with Donovan's murder.

"He's ill," Rosie said.

The barman was all sympathy, his imagination working overtime. "And he wants to see the journal before he – ? Is that what you meant by 'a matter of life or death?' Mr Donovan must have left a message for him in the journal."

The two nodded vehemently.

"Then of course you must have the suitcase. To tell you the truth, I'll be glad to get rid of it. I know it's only an old case, but it's been on my mind, especially after I heard Mr Donovan disappeared. I'd have given it to the police only I wanted to keep my promise. I hope the journal brings some comfort to your father."

They thanked him over and over and waited, weak with relief, while he went to fetch the suitcase from the stores. When he returned he spent some minutes carefully wiping away the dust from the surface. Then with a flourish, he handed it to them, his look of anticipation changing to one of disappointment when, instead of opening the case and revealing the contents, they thanked him once more and hurried from the pub.

Under a streetlamp they forced the lock with Patrick's penknife. Wrapped up in a bundle of clothes was the ledger Rosie had seen once before in the junk shop. She groaned, "This is just a pile of numbers. It's an account book."

But Patrick was turning every page. "No, Rosie. It's not. Look at the back."

They scanned the last quarter of the large notebook.

Excitement mounting, they could hardly breathe. "This is proof!" Patrick whispered. Then he shouted, "We've got Reddin!" And he danced up and down with joy.

The pages plainly detailed how Michael Donovan came to be in Reddin's debt, how Reddin was involved in the black market, how he wanted to get his hands on the company and how he threatened murder, saying he could kill and bury Donovan and put the blame on his partner. The journal even mentioned the gist of the letter to Reddin, the one the police thought went to Edward.

"If he knew his life was in danger, why didn't he do something about it?" Rosie was puzzled.

"He gives the reason here: *The police will take me for a rambling drunkard. After all, no harm has yet come to me. But if it should, then they cannot ignore this record.*"

For a few moments they felt sorry for the dead man, but then happiness took over. Edward would soon be free.

Patrick linked Rosie's arm in his and with a wild whoop he whirled her round the pavement.

Chapter 18

Time was on a rollercoaster now and there was no problem finding a way to fill it. They raced towards the police station. Almost there, they stopped to catch their breath, not wanting to arrive gasping and unable to explain. Leaning against the wall they took long draughts of air and slowly recovered. They were ready to go in when they saw a bowed figure coming down the hill.

"It's Wilson, the Englishman," Patrick said. "He doesn't look very happy."

"He must be coming in to make his statement," Rosie said. "We should talk to him."

The man was so taken up with his own bleak thoughts he didn't notice the two standing in his path till he bumped into them.

"Excuse me," Rosie said. "Aren't you Mr Wilson? We saw you last night in Howth."

Even in the moonlight they could see Wilson go pale. The reasons for his presence in Howth had not been law-abiding.

Patrick added casually, "That's right. We saw you talking

166

to Leonard Reddin. We heard every word too. Now my father has been charged with murder because of your plotting."

"Your father is Edward O'Neill?" the man croaked and when the boy nodded he muttered what sounded like an apology.

"There's no point saying sorry when you're going to tell lies about him!" Patrick's voice was harsh.

"What choice do I have?" Wilson pleaded. "If you heard everything, then you heard I've got a sick daughter. Very delicate she is. I ain't no good to her in prison, which is where I'll end up if I don't help Reddin. He'll make sure of it."

"So my father will be hanged to save you going to prison?" Patrick was blunt and the man had the grace to look ashamed.

He muttered, "I don't know if I can go through with this!"

"There's another way," Rosie told him and Wilson looked at her hopefully. "You could tell the truth about Reddin. And you could explain about your daughter. The judge might understand why you have to smuggle to pay for her. You might only get a little sentence. That kind of thing is always happening on telly and –"

Realising her mistake, she stopped. Wilson had listened attentively and now he said, "I don't know where this Telly place is, but I suppose the same thing could happen here. I'd be so glad to get Reddin off my back and out of my life. You just might have a good idea there."

"Oh, we have," Patrick was fervent. "And anyway, if you told lies about my father and he was hanged and then the truth came out later, you might be charged with his murder."

This awful possibility hadn't occurred to Wilson and he swallowed a number of times before he could speak. "I could be hanged as well," he whispered, "and Molly would be an orphan, her days numbered. Three lives destroyed."

"And Reddin would be rich and free," Rosie added.

The Englishman looked at them, suddenly straightening up. "I don't know how I ever got involved with that villain, but now is the time to be rid of him. Let's go into the station. I'll tell what I know and that vermin will get what's coming to him!"

The other two whooped with delight. Now they told him about the journal. He looked at them, puzzled, "Why didn't you say so at the very start? I wouldn't have gone in there to tell lies if I'd known you'd proof against Reddin. They'd have me for perjury or conspiracy or something."

"Why should we save you if you wouldn't save my father?"

Wilson took a deep breath, "Fair enough. I can understand that. What are we waiting for? Let's clear up this mess." And he strode into the police station, a weight off his shoulders.

As it turned out, it would be the next day before Edward was released.

While the three made their statements in Whitehall police station and the journal was produced, examined and noted, Edward was in the Dublin Mountains, deep in the forest.

He watched with awful sadness as the police, guided by

Reddin, set out lanterns on the forest floor and began to dig. Moonbeams shimmered through the trees and gleamed on Edward, setting him apart. Reddin stood in the shadows as though afraid to show his features in case they revealed the dark void of his spirit.

Their faces grim in the lantern light, the police set about the grisly task of digging up the murdered man. The grave was deep and it took them some time. No one spoke. The silence was broken by the clang of a spade catching a stone or the thump of soil as it hit the ground. Now and again the leaves rustled and an owl hooted. Otherwise the night was still.

Edward thought he had never witnessed such a terrible scene. He had met death before in the Great War, but not that of a friend in circumstances where he stood accused of his murder. Even death in battle was better than this. Michael Donovan had had no comrades when he'd met his end, no one to give the rallying cry, no one to look out for him, no chaplain to comfort his dying moments or give him a final blessing. And he'd had no friend to mourn his passing.

His death had been of the loneliest kind.

And, as the police lifted the body, wrapped in old sacking, Edward stepped forward and spoke clearly, "I promise you, Michael, justice will be done."

In the shadows, Reddin laughed, but the laughter was nervous.

Carefully and respectfully the police laid the body on a stretcher and brought it down the hillside to where an ambulance waited. The lanterns bobbed and weaved past the stacked turf and trenches, past the burnt-out cottage.

They heard the cry of the curlew as silently they settled back into the police cars and set off once again for the city.

And late that night while Rosie and Patrick were back home telling Maria all that had happened, her husband Edward was in the police station. Now the attitude of the gardai was apologetic rather than accusing. This time they listened and took his statement respectfully. This time Reddin was the accused.

It took the villain some hours to realise the game was lost. He twisted and turned, lying and bluffing, by turns furious and dismayed. He acted the innocent. He pretended sorrow over Michael Donovan's death and indignation at the notion that he, Reddin, could be thought guilty of such a crime.

But the police produced the journal and the Englishman's statement and then it was all up. Reddin could not slither away from the proof.

By dawn he realised his best chance was to admit guilt, then try to find an excuse that the judge would take into account. The police told him he would do his case no harm if he confessed and "those youngsters don't have to appear at a murder trial". To try and save his skin, Reddin confessed.

By six am as Edward walked home, a free man, justice done, his heart singing, Leonard Reddin pondered his fate with terror and hoped against hope that he would escape execution.

Chapter 19

Edward's arrival was greeted with many hugs and much delight.

Maria was tearful when she thought of what might have happened. Patrick put all his feelings into wild shouts and jumps of joy. Rosie thought she would never stop smiling. Edward himself kept thanking the two of them for what they'd done. "I'm proud of you, both. It was a brave thing to follow Reddin to Howth and it was clever to work out that the journal was in *The Cat and Cage*. Others might have given up when I was arrested, but you went back over everything!"

"That was Rosie's idea," said Patrick, a little embarrassed. He had never before seen his father in such an emotional state.

"But it was your idea to ask the barman who he was keeping the case for," Rosie said. "That was brilliant. We'd never have got the journal except for that."

Maria made a cooked breakfast and for an hour or more they discussed every detail. Gradually the excitement drained away, to be replaced by exhaustion. It had been a long night.

"I think we should rest," Edward said looking at their weary faces. I'll go in to the office after lunch. Now, I don't know about the rest of you, but I'm off to bed."

The others followed suit.

This time, when Rosie woke up she wasn't swamped by a feeling of dread. Instead she had a wonderful sense of freedom. There was nothing left for her to do except enjoy her last full day in 1943. For a while she lay there, thinking of everything that had happened and how it had all turned out right in the end. Then she wondered if she'd ever see Patrick again. Would he be alive in 2001? What age would he be?

Lazily she looked at her watch. It was three o'clock in the afternoon! She couldn't believe it. This was Edward's birthday and there was a party to prepare. Why was she still lying in bed?

Racing downstairs she found Maria and Mrs Kennedy in the kitchen, sitting by the gas stove, having a cup of tea. Through the window, in the back garden, she could see Patrick and Macker, playing Jackstones. "There's no way I'm going out there," she thought. "Macker'd have a great laugh when I wouldn't get past the first move."

Instead she joined the two women.

"Well, Rosie dear, I heard all about your exploits. Aren't you a great wee person altogether?"

Rosie could hardly agree, but Mrs Kennedy was only warming up and she poured the girl a cup of tea. "I believe Patrick and yourself were a great help to poor Mr O'Neill. Isn't that right?"

This time Rosie felt a nod was okay.

"Well, amn't I telling you now? You and young Patrick make a great team."

As bad luck would have it, at that moment Patrick saw Rosie through the window. He waved and smiled and did a little dance to say hello.

"Will you look at that now!" Mrs Kennedy teased. "He's so happy to see you. And why wouldn't he be? It's not every young man that has such a nice wee girlfriend!"

Rosie spluttered into her tea, her face growing beetroot as she choked. The woman pretended to notice nothing, but winked at Maria, who thought the girl had suffered enough. "Mrs Kennedy brought the morning newspaper," she said. "Look what it says. The story's out of date, but no doubt it will be corrected in the next edition."

Hiding her red face behind the paper, Rosie read the familiar words:

BUSINESSMAN CHARGED WITH MURDER

Yesterday evening, the businessman Edward O'Neill was arrested on suspicion of the murder of Michael O'Donovan, who disappeared one year ago.

She knew the rest off by heart and folded the newspaper. Not wishing to appear uninterested, she said, "May I keep this to read later?"

"Of course, dear," Mrs Kennedy said.

Rosie discovered that Maria and Patrick had been up for some time and, with the neighbour's help, had already prepared most of the food for the party.

Around tea-time they pulled the living-room table out

and extended it. From the flour they'd bought in *Pay an' Take*, Maria had made a birthday cake for Edward, with his name in coloured icing. This was given pride of place on the table, beside a huge jug of gin and tonic. Around these were placed bowls of popcorn and crisps, chocolate orange slices, plenty of fruit and all the cans of coke. Neighbours sent in cakes and scones they'd cooked from their rations. The table groaned with good things.

The curtains were drawn and everyone squeezed into the living-room, except Patrick who was sent to spot Edward's arrival. As soon as he saw his father in the distance, he rushed in and the room went quiet except for the odd giggle.

The front door opened.

"Maria! Hello! Anyone home?"

The doorknob turned. "God, it's dark! What's going on? Who's in here?"

"Happy Birthday to You!" someone sang and the rest joined in with great gusto, even Rosie who put everyone into the wrong key. But it didn't matter. The curtains were pulled back and neighbours crowded round to shake Edward's hand and wish him a special birthday after his terrible ordeal. When they'd finished, Rosie watched as he stood smiling, one arm around his wife, the other resting on Patrick's shoulder.

For a moment she felt excluded, not by those three, but by time. She didn't belong here and suddenly she was homesick, longing to see Mum and Dad and Gran, missing her friends Helena and David Byrne, missing the year from which she'd travelled.

But then the party got under way, with neighbours congratulating the two youngsters for their part in the drama.

Edward blew out the candles and the cake was cut and shared. When everyone had been provided with a drink, Edward raised a hand. "I'd like to say something." As people hushed each other, the conversation faded and Edward raised a glass. "First I'd like to toast our very special visitor, Rosie, and also my son, Patrick. If it weren't for them I'd be spending this birthday in a cell and the next one wouldn't bear thinking about. To Rosie and Patrick!"

And everyone shouted, "To Rosie and Patrick!"

When silence settled once more, Edward raised his glass again: "This time I'd like to toast my absent twin, Henry, who can't get home and has to spend his birthday in Switzerland."

"To Henry! Happy Birthday!" Everyone cheered and drank.

Conversation resumed and Rosie found herself the centre of much attention, answering questions about all that had happened the previous day.

Edward too was surrounded by well-wishers and was beginning to tire of telling the same story over and over. It was a while before he could seize on a lull to take himself off to the kitchen for a little peace.

Rosie noticed him leaving the room and went and fetched the present she'd brought for him. He was seated at the small table in the kitchen, savouring the quiet, when Rosie appeared with her gift. At first he was enthusiastic, his eyes lighting up at the idea of this "machine of the future". But as she showed him how it worked she could see his eagerness disappear. He tried to pretend he liked the Game-Player and the *Star Wars* discs, but she knew he wasn't really interested.

Disappointed, she said, "You used to love war games. I remember all your toy soldiers."

He smiled, a little sadly. "I liked toy battles. But then I joined the army and fought real ones. The reality had none of the wonder of make-believe. I thought war would be an adventure and instead it was a kind of torture."

"I'm sorry," Rosie said. "I brought you the wrong present."

"No," Edward was definite. "You gave me the best gift anyone could give when you came back. Without you I might not have my freedom. You gave me that!" He looked at the Game-Player. "It's a wonderful invention and if you don't mind I'll give it to Patrick. He showed great courage these last few days, just like you, and I'd like to reward him."

Rosie nodded. She was surprised by how serious Edward had become. A charge of murder would make anyone less light-hearted, she supposed, but this wasn't a temporary change. Edward's nature had altered and there was little trace of the boy she remembered.

As if catching her thoughts, he sighed, "When I see you, Rosie, I think what a pity it is we all have to grow up. Life doesn't have the same magic when you're an adult."

A silence followed until he changed the subject. "You're going home tomorrow?"

"Yes. I have to be back by tea-time."

Sadly he said, "We'll hardly meet again?"

When she did not answer, Edward said, "I can't complain. I'm lucky that you came back twice. It's great to hear about the future – even if Nelson's Pillar won't be there!" He smiled, but only briefly. "The trouble is, Rosie, you've become one of the family so easily. Perhaps that's because we're related. And now, just like the last time, when I've got used to thinking of you as part of our life, you're leaving, going somewhere none of us can follow, and you'll probably never come back here again, will you?"

"It gets harder every time," Rosie said. "Not just the journey to the past, though that too. Your father, Joseph, said his time-travelling stopped when he was fourteen. I'll soon be the same age. In a way I'll be glad if it all ends. I used to think it was the greatest adventure, but there are so many people I miss when I go home to my own time. People I know I'll never see again." She sighed, then added, "No, I won't come back here again. I haven't gone back to any time twice."

After a moment, Edward patted her hand and said, "I was wrong about you, Rosie. You're not the same person I met the last time. Oh, you may not look much older, but you're growing up."

"Growing up isn't that great," she said.

It was then the kitchen door opened and a neighbour looked in, wanting a word with Edward. Rosie returned to the party.

"I'm going home tomorrow afternoon," she told Maria.

"Well, it was a pleasure to have you here, young Rosie Hammond, and I'm grateful for all you did. I'm glad your mother is recovering well enough for you to go back and hopefully we'll see you soon again."

Mrs Kennedy overheard and couldn't resist her usual tease, "Ah now, Rosie dear, there's one young man who'll be right miserable when you're gone –"

The girl made her escape and ran into the same young man. His face fell when she told him she was leaving next day.

"Stay a while longer. I was just getting used to having a girl around."

"Thanks. I don't want to be something you have to get used to, like banana parsnips!"

"You're not. You're much better than banana parsnips!"

"I'm glad Mrs Kennedy can't hear your compliments."

They both grinned, then Patrick said resignedly, "I suppose you have to go home. Do you imagine that we'll ever meet again?"

It was then Rosie had a great idea and replied, "In 2001 I'm going to ask Mum to give a party for Gran, maybe at Christmas time. It would be nice if you could be there. Would you come to her party?"

Patrick did a rapid calculation. Solemnly he said, "I'll be seventy-one in 2001, but if I'm alive, no matter where I am, I'll contact you in Whitehall and I'll be there."

"Promise. No matter where you are."

"I swear."

Her spirits lifted and, with her goodbyes over, Rosie enjoyed the rest of the evening. Everyone was full of Reddin's villainy and Edward's narrow escape. They were also full of the war.

"Mussolini's finished," someone said. "Soon it will be Hitler's turn."

"And the allies are winning in Sicily and Africa," another added.

Edward's freedom, the victories of war and Mussolini's fall all became reasons for tremendous celebration so that for years afterwards neighbours remembered the party at number 35. They remembered the beautiful summer

weather, the wonderful food when for once rations were
forgotten and the supply of gin and tonic which had all the
adults tipsy;

They remembered the moonlight later on and everyone
singing Vera Lynn songs in the back garden, and that girl –
what was her name? – looking so sad when all of them
linked arms and sang:

> And I'll just say hello
> To the folks that you know
> Tell them you won't be long
> They'll be happy to know
> That as I saw you go
> You were singing this song:

> *We'll meet again, don't know where, don't know when,*
> *But I know we'll meet again some sunny day!*

Yes, it was a marvellous, happy night . . . at least until
someone asked the same wretched girl for a song . . .

At four o'clock next afternoon, Patrick's mother sent him
on a message to Mrs Doyle.

"Don't go till I get back," he'd told Rosie as he sped off.

But she had said her goodbyes the night before,
something she knew Edward had understood when he'd told
her, after the last of the guests had gone, "Have a good life,
Rosie. I won't come home from the office tomorrow to see
you off. I think we've said everything."

So now, while Maria was hanging clothes out to dry in
the back garden, Rosie left the house.

Outside the gate, by the tree, she set the date on her watch and thought of home. With all her power she concentrated on the house in Whitehall, on Mum and Dad, on her friends. She felt a shift in the space around her, but opened her eyes to the same scene: the horses and carts, the doctor's car at Mrs Doyle's; the paper boy with the early edition of the *Evening Herald* and the *Evening Mail*.

"Heddeldymail," he was yelling, "Businessman goes free! Read all about it. Heddeldlymail!"

She heard another shout and recognised Patrick's voice. *"Wait for me, Rosie! Don't go!"* She saw him running from Mrs Doyle's garden and then he was racing towards her. She closed her eyes again. Desperately she said, "I want to go back. I can't stay here! I must go home."

The last thing she heard before time changed was Patrick yelling, *"Goodbye, Rosie! Goodbye! See you in 2001! I'll be there in 2001, Rosie! I promise!"*

The words 'two thousand and one' echoed in the air and Rosie had a sense of the whole landscape fading away, and a new landscape forming, with different people and different, heavier sounds.

When she looked again, the horses and carts were gone, replaced by the roar of heavy traffic from the main road.

She was back.

Mum and Dad were there when she got home. Delighted to see her, they asked how she had enjoyed Connemara with Caroline. But her questions about Paris distracted them and they didn't notice the lack of answers.

Then Mum dropped a bombshell. Holding Caroline's letter, she said, "We can't make contact with her mobile.

We've been ringing the agency for the last while to check the number. But the line is engaged."

Aghast, Rosie said, "Why do you want to talk to her? What's wrong?"

"Nothing. We'd just like to thank her for taking you to Connemara."

Then her mum lifted the telephone and dialled and there was nothing Rosie could do.

"At last! It's ringing," Mum smiled.

Explaining who she was, she asked for Caroline's number, adding, "I want to thank her for the care she took of our daughter and especially for taking her on holiday."

Rosie closed her eyes and prayed. She heard her mum say, "Really! Rosie never told us that!" 'Oh God!' she thought. The game was up. The agency woman must know she'd never gone to Connemara.

"Is that right?" her mum said. "I hope everything goes well for Caroline. I'll have a word with Rosie. She really should have said."

She put the phone down and turned to her daughter, expression serious. "Why didn't you tell us?"

In a panic, Rosie couldn't say a word. How could she begin to explain where she'd really been?

"What did she not tell us?" Dad said.

"That we can't contact Caroline on her mobile. That she was offered a great job in Finland, minding a little boy for a very wealthy family, starting next week. She's gone for at least a year. Apparently she took the train up from Galway this morning and left Dublin airport this afternoon. Why on earth didn't you say something, Rosie, before I rang the agency?"

181

Overwhelmed with relief, the girl said truthfully, "You didn't give me any time to tell you. Before I could say anything, you were dialling."

Her mother accepted this with good grace.

"You're looking very tanned," Dad observed. "You must have had good weather for the week. I suppose you lazed around on the beach the whole time?"

"I did not," Rosie said. "I spread manure, dried turf on a bog, queued for food and did loads of housework!"

"Is that right?" Dad said with the total disbelief she'd expected. "And we weren't in Paris at all. We were on Mars."

The End.